Warthogs and Feathers

Warthogs and Feathers
The Editor Escapes the Pen

Linda Salisbury

McNeill Books

© 2025 Linda G. Salisbury

All rights reserved. No part of this book may be reproduced, stored in a retrieval system, or transmitted by any means, electronic, mechanical, photocopying, recording or otherwise, without written permission from the author. This a work of fiction. Any resemblance to persons or places is coincidental.

ISBN: 979-8-21853209-3
Library of Congress Control Number: 2024921811
Cover design: MarionDesigns

McNeill Books
Punta Gorda, Florida

1

"Damn the warthogs!" Their shiny bodies were coupled again in compromising positions.

Basil Randall Beale Jr. slouched in his office chair, which he had refused to surrender when interior decorators redesigned the editorial offices twelve years earlier. The worn chocolate-and-moss colored striped fabric didn't match the mauve-and-teal-accents selected by the publisher's wife. But after several semi-pleasant confrontations, and most specifically, his refusal to budge, the comfortable threadbare chair remained. He knew staff whispered in the outer office that it was just a short time until his retirement from Ozburn, Ozburn & Ozburn, and his chair would be discarded. In his favor of holding onto the status quo was his seniority and the fact that the chair was not visible when anyone was stopped at the front desk by the new receptionist, Samantha. Now there was just a month left, and only one more book to edit before he would close the glass door between his private office and young staff for the last time, and his chair would be quickly wheeled to the Dumpster. He hadn't decided yet what to do about the unwanted warthogs, a surreptitiously growing collection on his bookcase and desk.

Basil sifted through the detritus on his massive, scarred wooden desk—another piece of furniture he refused to relinquish until retirement. Unlike the modern poly-something ones that filled the large staff editing room, where college grads with English-lit majors and no understanding of basic punctuation or sentence diagramming, occassionally recommended manuscripts for his consideration, his spacious desk had useful drawers. Drawers for red pens and pencils (items almost obsolete in the computer workstations). Drawers for files and yellow legal pads. A drawers for concealing his leather-encased flask of bourbon, rarely used, but a staple from the past. Basil had erasers, adhesive tape . . . a small first-aid kit (used only once due to his careless hand gesture toward a spindle). On top of the piles of papers was a printout of the new manuscript, along with a flash drive. A mauve sticky note asked him to "please edit, preferably on screen. Stat!"

Hell no! None of that, he thought. *I will edit my last book as I did my first. Red pen or pencil marks, notes in the margin (some snide).* He pushed aside his dirt-brown coffee cup with the word BOSS printed in cream-colored letters; a gift from the paid interns and staff he would soon happily leave behind.

Basil glanced briefly through the large glass windows that separated him from staff cubicles. Would these young employees—most of them interns hoping for a higher-paying position—have loyalty to a single employer? Would they be lifers, staying with the firm long past the age when many acquaintances had retired? Not likely. They would be impatient to earn more and have greater benefits and would depart soon after being trained. Basil would have been willing to work until seventy or older, but he had felt pushed, albeit subtly, to retire at sixty-seven.

He turned to the title page, and sighed. It was another damn book with a cutsie title like *The Lighthouse Keeper's Daughter; The Astronaut's Aunt, The Sanitation Engineer's Wife.* How many best sellers or wannabees had that type of title? Too many. This one was about the worst he had ever encountered: *The Devine Royalty Social Club Queen's Son.* How did it get through the initial reading process with the editorial underlings? Basil lifted his red pen and firmly crossed it out. Bad title, he scribbled, as if that comment was necessary.

He wondered if the manuscript had been foisted on Ozburn, Ozburn & Ozburn by Evanna, a so-called literary agent known to Howard Ozburn III. The agent was the offspring of one of Howard's country club buddies, a girl with a crackle in her voice that was so popular and annoying these days. "Vocal fry," he'd read that they called it. He figured that Ozzie III was probably taken with its sound or her looks rather than smarts.

Basil twirled his pen, then had another sip of coffee, taking care not to let it dribble on the pristine manuscript. He studied the dusty wood-framed family photos behind his mug. Basil smiled at the image of his beautiful wife Shirley and their lovely daughter Amanda. They both had had thick blonde hair and blue eyes. He would pack the photos last. Basil was glad that neither of his progeny had gone into writing. It was almost impossible to have a book by an unknown be accepted at one of the established houses these days. And writers, tainted by the snobbery of writers groups, still labored under the misconception that big houses would pick them up, if they paid the right agent. He knew that most authors were self-publishing, and that much of the material was unedited and terrible.

Amanda, his youngest daughter—a surprise child to Basil and his second wife, Shirley—had expressed an interested in writing but fortunately, she had taken a job in marketing for Healthy, Wealthy & Wise Food Groups and seemed to be excelling at that. She'd begun writing a novel in third grade, but had never finished it nor had she shared it with the family. *Just as well, even if she had talent,* Basil thought. *She'd just be disappointed with the difficulties of becoming published now.*

He stared at the cubicles in the main room. It was possible that interns were working, but it was more likely that most of them were setting up online dates or seeing what was trending on social media. No matter. They could do what they pleased in a month when a yet-unnamed replacement would move into his space.

Basil turned to chapter one, looked at the clock, sighed and read:

> "What'cha snitchin, Ashly Belor?"
> She looked surprised, but not as much as he might expect. "Nun yer business," said Ash. "Besides, it's not snitchin when nobody wants it."
> "How do you know?" asked Dresden, positioning himself in front of her on the weedy path.
> "Nobody ever goes in there anymore. And me, I never went there more than once. Just today," she said.

Dresden didn't believe her. He'd seen her several times slinking out of the tall grass, looking this way and that, wiping the cobwebs out of her long brown hair that needed more than good combing. He had spotted her the last time when he had been slouched on a stump near the poplar tree and she didn't think anyone was looking. He had not only seen her, but he was sure she had stuffed her shorts pockets with things she found inside the old building. Now she had a lumpy pillowcase slung over her shoulder.

"Saw you before," said Dresden.

"Saw someone else," said Ash. "Now get outta my way."

Dresden didn't move. He was a year younger but a foot taller and heavy enough to play high school football if he had had the ambition.

Ash glared at him with pecan-colored eyes. "I suppose you want some stuff too," she said. "But why don't you get your own. You could go in there, unless yer a scaredy . . ."

Dresden interrupted, "I ain't scaredy. Just don't think anyone should . . ."

"If yer not scared, just go on in. I'm done there." Ash stepped toward him and this time Dresden moved aside. He could hear things rattling and banging in the pillowcase as she disappeared.

Dresden supposed it wouldn't hurt to have a look inside, but he wished he were wearing his sneakers to follow the overgrown weedy path. He hadn't planned to go this far to exercise his banged-up knee; flip-flops weren't much protection. It felt like bugs and ticks were crawling on his almost-bare feet and up his shins, where they could hide under the bandage wrap. He wondered how Ash could stand walking through the tall grass when you couldn't see snakes or spiders or especially prickers. It didn't take long for his silky gray shorts to be covered with stick-tights that he'd have to pick off before he threw them in the wash or they'd be attached forever like dark freckles. He knew the small dog that had followed him from home would be equally tagged with them.

> Dresden wasn't sure he was limping in the right direction when suddenly he found himself in a small clearing, an area that had once been a neatly mowed lawn. About fifty feet ahead was the building he knew Ash had been raiding: The Devine Royalty Social Club. The faded name painted purple with red letters and gold trim was still visible on a sign above door. He paused and surveyed the building that still had a reputation for being haunted.

Basil scribbled on a yellow pad. What kind of genre would this fit? Mystery, Southern, or Young Adult Book? Beginning isn't clear. The proposed back cover summary doesn't adequately explain. He did like Dresden's clothing—different than what he might have expected a novice to invent. Perhaps a writers group had provided suggestions to one of their members. Character names weren't bad either.

> Dresden wondered if the wooden floor still had a dark red stain from the last time that the Devine Royalty Social Club had been open, and if chairs were still flipped on their sides from when its members rushed away into the night. MaMa was among the runners, and so was aunt Poli.
> Who could forget that night! Hearing them burst through the front door of his home and then pretend nothing was wrong. Breathing hard, and without their high heels, they walked quickly and quietly to Poli's small bedroom behind the kitchen and shut the door. The women didn't seem to notice that Dresden and little brother, Bodie, had turned on the TV in their absence, instead of doing their homework. It was just extra baby-stuff worksheets, from Mrs. Spencer with the nose whiskers that she tweezed when she thought no one in the class was looking.
> "They're home early. Something happened at the club," whispered Bodie, picking up his pencil stub.
> "Yeah. Maybe they saw a ghost," said Dresden. He dug at a mosquito bite on his ankle. Maybe Rufus, he's the only one bad enough to haunt."
> "Not Rufus," said Bodie. "Maybe old Salami." He rightly knew that mispronouncing Salomay's name would make his brother snort. He was not disappointed.

> The brothers heard the bedroom door creak open and MaMa tell her sister that she'd be right back and out the front door she went. But she wasn't back by the time Aunt Poli, in her nightgown, the faded one with tiny yellow butterflies, sneaked into the living room and grabbed the TV remote and the unfinished worksheets.
>
> "I heard MaMa tell you very clearly to do your worksheets first. Here it is bedtime and here they are almost blank. Did you not hear her?"
>
> "Yes, Ma'am," Dresden said, and Bodie quickly echoed.
>
> "Then do it. I'm sitting right here until you're done."
>
> "Where's MaMa?" asked Dresden.
>
> "Out," said Aunt Poli, and the fearsome worried look on her face told them not to ask anything else. MaMa did not come home before they went to bed, and in the morning, the haggard look on her face made them quickly eat their toast without a word and then hurry down the lane to catch the bus after breakfast.
>
> When the women did not return to the Devine Royalty Social Club the following Tuesday evening, or any Tuesday after that, which they had done as they had for as long as Dresden could remember, he finally asked MaMa why.
>
> She frowned, didn't answer, and sent him to the cellar for a quart of canned peaches.

At least the author has run spell-check and uses proper punctuation, Basil noted. *Location seems to be in the South, maybe Georgia.* He was mildly caught up in the story, but had questions. *If the place has been vacant for so long, why would that girl be removing things now? In his urban neighborhood, anything left unsecured would be gone and hawked in ten minutes.*

Basil glanced at his staff again. Samantha was sitting on Lisa's desk and both women were studying a smart phone. *Probably texting boyfriends,* he thought, *or ordering lunch.* Basil had a flip phone, and used it only in an emergency. Amanda had given him a smart phone for Christmas, but he hadn't bothered to activate it. Who needed all that constant communication? He sighed, and twirled his red pen, then turned his attention to the manuscript.

 Even though he could no longer hear things clattering in the pillowcase, Dresden suspected that Ash was watching, perhaps even following him. That girl had no business going to the old club building. She hadn't moved in down the road until years after the members ran out into the dark. As far as he knew, none of her kin had been members of either Full Royalty or the Outer Court. MaMa had been the queen several times and Aunt Poli was her attendant for least four of-five of her reigns. Outsiders, even family members, weren't supposed to know anything. The members were so secretive that Dresden figured they had taken a blood oath. But weeks before that Tuesday night, Dresden and Bodie had found MaMa's scrapbook on the top shelf of her closet when they were looking for Christmas presents. MaMa had taped in photographs taken at balls and meetings, and tucked in glittery programs, plus what looked like a secret code folded up like a paper-chain doll.

 MaMa had even gotten the boys' father, Hiram, all dressed up and photographed for the Queens Holiday Ball. His father cussed the next day about how stupid he felt wearing a fake crown. Dresden didn't remember seeing his dad putting on the long, fur-trimmed robe at the house before walking to the club, so he figured that members must have stored the costumes for the men at the clubhouse. Dresden wondered if the costumes were still there or if someone, like Ash, had thefted them, as MaMa would say.

 It wasn't that anyone would ever use that building again. It would crumble in time like barns and sheds and the small log hunting cabins in the mountain woods. First a piece of tin roof would twist in a strong winter wind and snow or rain would creep under to soak the beams. A board would rot and fill with mealy bugs or digger bees, ants and termites. A kid would break another window. Floorboards would sag and become as holey as deli cheese. The plastic police tape that had once surrounded the building was mostly gone—snipped into small souvenirs by the curious.

After he and Bodie had returned a time or two, Dresden lost interest. He had found another abandoned buildings to explore in the neighborhood—a rural area becoming more commercial as increasing traffic flooded the new bypass.

In the soft rot of a cabin he had examined three years later, Dresden found buttons, rusty bent nails, pennies and pieces of broken bowls. He wondered why people left things behind unless they were running away in the night. In another abandoned tenant farm he had found a spoon with the initials CK etched in. He stuck it in his back pocket to show Bodie, but the spoon fell out.

The woodsy setting reminded Basil the location of a place they had rented for three weeks one summer when Amanda was about twelve. Basil wasn't keen on "roughing it," but Shirley had insisted that would be a good opportunity to get away from the city and bond with each other. She had been seeing a therapist at the time who was into bonding. *All crap,* Basil thought and he finally said so, but Shirley was insistent.

The decades-old log cabin was the right size for three people and it included fishing tackle (a small pond was within walking distance), and four Adirondak chairs in the yard. Amanda quickly claimed a hammock strung between two large pines. Shirley and Amanda created bonding experiences—such as foraging together for wild berries and mushrooms. As time went on, the bonding involved only the two of them. Basil preferred solitude and eating from canned food they had purchased at a Southern supermarket with an absurd porcine name, rather than risking death by unknown mushroom varieties. Only experts knew which kinds were safe and which would kill you even if you sautéed them in $100 a bottle olive oil from California that Shirley had bought in a specialty shop.

The Devine Royalty Social Club should be allowed to collapse like the rest of the old buildings, a normal death, as the weeds and vines helped pull it down in private. Then a vagrant might light a fire and the rubble would burn. That would sure be better than to have it bulldozed for the new Piggly Wiggly shopping center that folks hoped would be built there along with a sandwich shop and drug store. Old things should just die naturally.

It had been a while since Dresden had been to the club. His mother and the other members had warned youngsters to stay away, but of course every kid in town had gone right out there for a look, their imaginations gone wild. Every red stain had to be blood showing the madness of that night, they figured, as they compared theories. A creak or skittering sound would be enough to send them running with tales about having been chased by the ghost. As time went on, the excitement of sneaking over to the clubhouse wore off except for Halloween. Someone always claimed to have been spooked by a haunting at midnight.

As he limped back there now, Dresden wondered if the front doors were still wide open and chairs overturned or had someone like Ash, who had no business being there at all, had moved everything around, took what they wanted, and shut the doors.

Dresden swatted a mosquito on his sweaty neck. He couldn't hear Ash anymore, and after glancing around to make sure she wasn't silently watching, he pushed through the tall grass that she had flattened moments earlier, and traced her path to the club.

No harm, he thought, *in having another look.*

He thought back to his first visit when he tried to get his brother to go with him. But Bodie had refused to go back the day after "The Night." He scrinched his eyes and shook his head so that long shocks of hair fell over his face and refused to budge. Finally, Dresden shrugged and whistled for Custard, whose legs looked like they should have been attached to a squirrel rather than a dog. Custard stretched and waddled after Dresden. Her nose was good, but she wasn't much for running. Eventually she'd sniff him out if he got too far ahead.

"If they're looking for me, say that I jus gone for berries," Dresden told his younger brother.

Bodie barely moved. It was enough for Dresden to know that he heard.

That was years earlier. Custard, wrapped in a frayed blue Fred Flintstone bath towel, had been under a rock for four years, next to Twix, a small yellow feral cat that came out of the woods and died three days later. MaMa wrapped Twix in a dish towel and tucked her in a size-twelve shoe box. "Too bad we didn't see the BB hole," she said. "She dint come up close enough for us to tend her."

Now Aunt Poli's pug-mix, a descendant of Custard, snuffled behind him in the clearing. Dresden was glad Ash hadn't seen the dog they called Grunt. She would have sniggered that a person Dresden's size would be seen in the company of something that looked like a miniature shaggy pig.

Basil was surprised that he found the animal's description amusing. Everybody had stories about their pets. Early in their marriage, he and Shirley had purchased a fluffy puppy that was supposed to be a purebred Yorkie. It looked more like a poodle-mix and snuffled loudly when it trotted after them on walks. Basil was embarrassed by people's questions about the dog's health. He had no answer other than to say the obvious, that the dog was born that way.

Who would have mowed the clearing around an abandoned building? Nobody had used the club house for years, at least so far as Dresden knew. One day he went back there without Bodie, a few months after that terrible night, the Devine Royalty Social Club building was still painted up and the bushes were neatly trimmed. Wooden shutters weren't askew, like now. He didn't tell Bodie that he hadn't gone inside, but just peered in the window, one that was open to let in cool night air during the club's meetings. The door had been open, but Dresden hadn't been sure what might be in there, so he walked around until he found some bricks and piled them up until he could see in. Custard had growled—a long worried growl that stuck in her throat and rumbled to her back where a ridge of fur rose like a worn-out toothbrush.

He shook his finger at her, hoping she'd be quiet. He could see a dark red stain on the floor. Chairs were toppled. Books and papers scattered. Something like a crown near the front of the room where a long table was on a raised platform. Books and papers were spread on it. Flags at either end. Pictures of club queens—he was sure he recognized MaMa's face, serious but smiling just a little, under the crown. He heard a creaking, maybe steps and decided he'd seen enough. He stepped off the bricks, but one fell striking another and Dresden bolted with old Custard panting behind him as they ran back home through the brush.

Now, here was Grunt laying in the weeds near the edge of a small cleared area. At least she appeared to be laying down but she might be sitting. Dresden was never quite sure. He stopped and considered the look of things.

The club's front door was still open, but the window where Dresden had rested his chin years ago as he peered in was closed; the pile of bricks stacked neatly to one side.

Dresden didn't need the bricks now to look inside, but what would the harm be of just walking in the front door as he was sure Ash had done many times?

The stains he remembered were hardly distinguishable from the darkened plank flooring. The chairs were stacked against the wall where he had peered through the window, their red velvet seats chewed by something, and gold fringe torn.

The pictures of MaMa and the other queens were no longer hanging on the front wall. Remnants of the dishes were swept to one side with the good china in one pile and broken pieces in the other. There was no sign of the silver or candlesticks, or the books and papers that Dresden remembered seeing. Grunt snuffled toward a room to the right side of the meeting hall and Dresden cautiously followed. It was the kitchen. A few pots were in the sink and pans were on the counter but if someone had fixed a banquet the night that the members ran out screaming, a lot of utensils and pans had to be missing. Maybe Ash took them. Grunt found something near the sink to chew and Dresden didn't stop her.

He remembered how Aunt Poli and MaMa made their favorite casseroles—his aunt added wild mushrooms—and desserts once a month when the Devine Royalty Social Club had a special dinner—the first Tuesday, maybe. Other nights, it was just cookies and sweet tea and sometimes they brought the extras home. But on that last night MaMa and Aunt Poli got all gussied up, as his mother put it, and they were having a caterer. "Fit for a queen," she said.

If Dresden had been paying attention that night he would remember what the occasion was. Was it another coronation? His mother and Aunt Poli never spoke of it, at least so as you could hear.

He hoped Grunt wouldn't get sick from whatever she was chewing. She would whine and cough and puke, then need to eat grass. Dresden wasn't done poking around. He noticed a pantry closet next to the refrigerator. Somebody had raided it probably before the mice got to the remaining bags and boxes. Recipe cards—some with footprints covering the ingredient lists were scattered on the pantry floor. Nothing worth keeping. He yanked open the refrigerator door and was immediately sorry. The food had decayed years ago leaving unidentifiable remains on plates.

Basil rubbed his temples. A filthy refrigerator. How many times had he read manuscripts that described one? If authors were writing about what they knew, and he wasn't sure that was often the case, many must have encountered someone who had not dealt with leftovers before they glowed with mold.

Shirley's mother saved small containers of three peas until they were fuzzy, or chunks of meat that turned mossy. Butter, well, he'd rather not think about its taste. Shirley claimed that her mother, who saved everything, was a product of the Great Depression. That would explain the hundreds of packets of sugar that they found in her pantry, as well as tiny foil-covered tubs of jelly, lifted surreptitiously, as if the waitress hadn't noticed, from local restaurants. Basil had put his foot down about moving them from his mother-in-law's pantry to their own after she had entered a nursing facility at age ninety-one.

Behind the door to the meeting room, a pile of papers caught Dresden's eye, especially when he saw some were stained with dark reddish-brown like old leather. Dresden knelt for a closer look.

"What'cha doing, boy?" asked a voice he didn't recognize.

Grunt attempted to bark a warning but instead choked, cried, coughed and puked.

"Going to clean up that dog's mess?" asked the voice.

Dresden nodded. He couldn't see where the voice was coming from. He tried to stand, but hands pushed him down.

"I asked you questions."

"Sorry, mister," said Dresden in a hoarse whisper. "I was just looking around. MaMa and her sister used to come to meetings here."

"So? That give you the right to trespass?"

"No, sir. I didn't think this place belonged to nobody."

"That girl a friend of yours?"

"Nope." The hands tightened. "I mean, no, sir."

"She's been helping herself, but it's easier to clean out."

"Could you please, let me up? My knees hurt," said Dresden. He could hear Grunt coughing in the yard. The dog was too stupid to go for help like Lassie would have done. Instead Dresden could die in the kitchen—in this abandoned social club—and no one would miss him for days. And he hadn't even had a chance to read any of the papers on the floor in front of him. Maybe when Grunt was done chewing grass, she'd come back in and snarl and bite the voice's shins. That wasn't likely. After Grunt ate grass she usually took a nap and farted. Useless dog.

The hands released him. "Now sit over there and face the sink," said the voice, "and we'll talk."

Dresden awkwardly got to his feet and moved to a stool near the island in the center of the room.

He faced the sink not daring to glance behind him.

"So," said the voice, "what were you looking for in those papers?"

"I just saw them there and maybe some blood and I just wanted to know . . ."

"Wanted to know what?" Dresden heard a lighter flick and he could smell a cigarette.

"Uh, what happened that night, I guess. No one ever talks about it. Just wondered, that's all."

"And why should they?"

"Something bad must have happened. They all ran away screaming," said Dresden. Sweat was dampening his neck, red muscle T-shirt and silky shorts. "My ma was queen and maybe she left something here when she ran off," he said.

"Like what?"

"I don't know." He wiped his brow.

"Maybe she already came back for it," said the voice.

Dresden hadn't thought of that possibility.

"You'd better go now," said the voice. "And think carefully about never returning. I'm putting up trespass signs this afternoon."

"Yes, sir."

"And don't forget the dog puke."

Basil removed his wire-frame glasses and wiped the lenses on a mouse-gray microfiber cloth printed with his eye doctor's name and phone number in type large enough to read without his glasses. His lenses had become thicker through the years as his vision worsened. He preferred to read at his desk with illumination either from the brief sunlight that squeezed between the tall buildings, or with light from his brass desk lamp with a green shade—a gift from his first wife, Margo, when he started with Ozburn House as a galley runner. That was what he privately called the non-editing job. It sounded more important than admitting he wouldn't be editing or proofing, just carrying galleys from one reader to another. But he had a small table in the corner near Princeton Michael Farmington, third vice president of acquisitions for the publishing house. When Basil wasn't running errands, he listened carefully to Princeton's conversations about the books under consideration. While collecting red pencils that others had dropped or discarded, Basil moved up. He was seen as a thoughtful, quiet, studious sort, never participating in office intrigue or politics, and one who preferred solitude to socializing. His proofreading was impeccable.

Then, three years into his career as an editor, he was summoned to OMO's office.

"How could this happen?" Old Man Ozburn, referred to as OMO, repeated the question in case Basil hadn't heard the first time. OMO shoved an open book across the desk.

Basil stared at the dedication in astonishment. He had no recollection that he had ever seen the book or page after his cursory look at what he considered a bad book about a vulgar politician, who during his life had certainly pissed away funds, public safety regulations, and opportunities for leadership in the world, and respect. He had pissed off his wife by having an affair, with not one but three women. Lobbyists loved him and he had been reelected four times, before going to his great reward. In private and public life, the man had pissed off many people. Basil's lips threatened to quiver.

"I have no idea," said Basil, which was not what OMO nor the firm's attorney want to hear.

"We'll have to discard the first run, reprint, and also settle. An apology won't work. But, Basil, I expect more of you. Don't let this happen again. Shoddy oversight on your part."

"Yes, sir." Basil was afraid his legs might buckle beneath him as he pushed back the conference room chair and tried not to seem too desperate to leave the room. When he reached his office, he needed to think about what to say to his staff and his exact tone of voice. He also secreted a copy of the advance reader's edition. It might be valuable someday. It was one of the first things he had packed and taken home to his closet as retirement neared.

He reflected on how this incident had shaped his management style, and yet staff didn't appreciate him. He hadn't yelled or fired anyone when those first copies were sent to reviewers. Stacks of first copies of the first edition were already in the distributor's warehouse ready to ship to bookstores. Unfortunately, none of the copy editors had noticed that in this biography of an unpopular corrupt congressman, the dedication said that he had "pissed away" unexpectedly.

No, Basil had not gone on a rant, like his predecessor would have done. Instead, he loosened his tie, strode into the editing staff area, cleared his throat, and announced a new rule. There would be no further use of "passed away" in any book passing through the doors of Ozburn and Ozburn. "Henceforth, people will simply die," he said firmly.

Silence had greeted his edict. No one took notes. No one suggested other alternatives that they might substitute, such as "Went to his great reward," "Left us peacefully to meet His Maker." "Is riding his Harley in Heaven." Not a suggestion of "Sped to the Pearly Gates," or "Peacefully crossed the beautiful river," or "Took the Lord's hand and followed the bright light with his cat." Basil retuned to his office and closed the door rather than watch his staff's reactions—that were likely holding back laughter, as they had no sense of the gravity or cost of recalling a press run of 300,000 books because of a threatened lawsuit by the congressman's ex-wife and the congressman's biographer. Their attorneys had called Old Man Ozburn (Howard II) within ten minutes of receiving their advance copies, OMO had summoned Basil to the conference room.

A day after that meeting with staff, the first of the ugly ceramic warthogs arrived. Basil had no idea why. Ugly. Tusks. Skin, plastic bristles and large warts above the eyes, and on the lower jaw. Sideburns. They had beards like shovels. He threw away the first two, but more appeared and more. He gave up and pushed the sounders, as the herd was called, to the side of his desk, where they spread.

No, he would not be sorry to leave the current staff, who admired pranks that had been pulled on him through the years, probably in reaction to his silence and sometimes taciturn communications with his employees, such as the "pissed way" incident decades earlier.

There was the time that he went on vacation, well, it was a working vacation, to a book trade show in Miami. While Shirley shopped and lounged on the beach, Basil wandered the booths to see what the competition's new winter line of books would include.

When he returned to work a week later he discovered that everything in his office had been turned upside down, including his desk and the lamp with a green shade. Books, pictures, his growing collection of horrible miniature warthogs.

He grimaced and stared through the glass panes at his staff, all apparently hard at work, all suppressing mischievous grins. Why was this so amusing?

Perhaps it was retaliation for his annual cleaning of Arcade's desk. Despite the man's proof-reading brilliance, Harold Arcade was the worst slob that Basil had ever worked with. Basil had "inherited him" when he took the editor's position thirty-five years earlier when smoking inside was still allowed. Arcade smoked three-packs a day, unfiltered, and filled his souvenir ashtray in the shape of Texas with gray ashes and butts no larger than his yellowed fingernails. The map imprinted on the ashtray's surface was never been visible until Basil scrubbed it ten minutes after Arcade, a dour, unwashed man, had left. Privately Basil thought that the odor of the constant cigarette smoke was preferably to Arcade's body's. Basil had never known what to do about enforcing dress codes, so he simply tried to be a good example by wearing a tweed jacket, pressed pants and shirt, and alternating ties. Polished brown shoes, laces tied neatly, of course. Shirley tried to help him by providing manly deodorant each year for Arcade's office Christmas stocking. There was no indication that it had been used.

Arcade was never inspired by his boss's example. Every year he left on his long-anticipated musical vacation at the International Advanced Beginners Banjo Camp, bidding his fellow employees a cheery farewell. He would return to find not only his ashtray had been dumped of its volcanic mound of butts and ash, then cleaned and sanitized, but also that his desk had been straightened up and polished. Arcade would sink into a depression that lasted until the following summer.

When Arcade died under suspicious circumstances involving his electric banjo and an emu, Basil asked for a few minutes of silence in the editing room. Rather than scrub the ashtray one more time, he sent for a janitorial trash barrel and shoveled Arcade's personal effects (he had no family) into it, then sprayed the surrounds with air freshener.

The hiring process for a replacement did not go well. Basil was so determined to find someone who met his private dress code—namely someone who was clean and didn't smoke—that he was stuck with candidates who had gone to school to become writers or copy editors, but had no sense about the profession. They don't know a colon from a tilde, he fumed. A dangling participle from a metaphor. A semaphore from a semicolon. He smiled at his own grim humor.

But that was years ago, before computers, security badges and an abundance or unpaid interns replaced mostly reliable staff.

Other than himself, there was only one person left from that era in his editing room and that was Manford Hooker. Perhaps The rarely seen Hooker would be the one to give a toast or a roast at Basil's farewell party, if there was to be one. Certainly cheerful Samantha would be directed to order a cake, hopefully chocolate with coconut frosting, and the Ozzies, the founder's children, would make a surprise appearance to thank Basil for his many faithful years of service, and they'd probably hand him an envelope with a little extra cash. Amanda and Shirley would also pop in to wish him well and to be featured in professional photographs taken by that new person in marketing. They'd be given a copy of the picture and would use it in their Christmas letter. Then he'd have to think of something humble and kind to say, to make sure that his soon-to-be rudderless staff, would panic when they realized his astute leadership would no longer be available to them the next day.

Amanda would help carry his three boxes of personal items, including the carefully wrapped warthogs (she insisted on keeping them), and he would head out the door for happy hour at Shirley's favorite tapas restaurant. She would order for him because he could never remember what he liked there.

Amanda had become almost a total vegan; she almost always ordered vegan food because she said it made her feel like she was saving not only animals but also the health of curds. "Modern wait staffs, although they don't always show it, have a deep respect for vegans," Amanda added, "because they know vegans have strong principles."

Shirley sighed, and ordered beef tartare. "I have deep principles too," she said, "but I like meat. I don't know where I went wrong raising you, Amanda. You used to be so, well, normal. Besides what's wrong with eggs and cheese?"

Before Amanda could jump in and quote one of the many social media studies about how goats and cows don't like to be milked and even free-ranging hens should be encouraged not to lay eggs (it all had to do with roosters that had no self-control) Basil had abruptly interjected that he liked vegetables and meat, hoping to stave off a family argument in public.

Basil thought, *I hope Amanda doesn't get involved with catering choices for my party. Her vegan cake didn't turn out very well for her friend Harvey's birthday. Maybe because it was both vegan and gluten free. The frosting looked liked cilantro.* Yes, only a month to go, this one final book, then the farewell party. Then what? He had no ideas for his retirement. He didn't want to think about it. It would not involve reading, at least not for a while.

Amanda and Shirley had listed suggestions.

"Dad, you should take up gardening. Build a greenhouse so you can do it year-round. Plant herbs and salad greens to sell to restaurants. Vegan Express would buy them."

Basil did not recall responding. Nor did he answer Shirley when she suggested that they travel to Iceland. "Everybody is going there," she said.

"Or, you could take up Polish online, or learn how to knit. Lots of men do that," suggested Amanda. "Or you could apply for a job at Healthy, Wealthy & Wise. We have openings in the mail room and billing." She looked at his stony face. "Just kidding, Dad. You'll think of something."

Basil didn't want to think of something or anything. He knew what to do at his job. He had no idea how to handle an endless vacation. He wondered when he had become depressed and feeling unable to find joy and purpose in his job and life in general. Could it be when he reached fifty the mid-life crisis that other men bragged about had passed him by? No new red convertible or gold chains? No taking up golf? His gloom spread around the office as the interns seemed less interested in working, and he mostly kept to himself behind those glass windows.

He turned to a clean page in his yellow legal pad and planned to list questions he had about the final manuscript. Instead he doodled a stick figure with a fishing pole at the top of an erupting volcano then scribbled it out.

2

It was a twenty-minute bus ride from their three-bedroom apartment to the office in typical congested traffic. During the years that Shirley found city life novel and unthreatening, she and Basil happily lived in the same place. But after 9/11, she was constantly braced for disaster. Shirley was a Plan B person, always having an alternative route or plan in mind. Basil thought that secondary plans were unnecessary—a waste of mental energy.

"I'm on my way," he said that morning. "Have an early meeting with the Ozzies."

"Are you taking the bus?" Shirley called from the bathroom.

"Yes."

"What if the construction snarls everything again today? I saw it on the news last night. You might want to take the subway. Or better yet, Uber."

"I'll be fine."

"That's what you said yesterday and you were an hour late."

"Not to worry."

"But, darling, you don't want to jeopardize your retirement by being let go, or whatever they call it, in the last few weeks. I hear about that all the time. Then what will you do?"

"I'll be fine," muttered Basil. She had a point. He had no Plan A for his life. For years Shirley had been begging him to prepare for a downsized publishing company, or having his position eliminated. She worried that even more authors would simply submit books to be printed online without editing as a cost-savings measure. Basil's careful editing, and judgement about what should be required for publication, would not be needed.

"Plan B. Develop other skills. Learn how to design pages or covers. Anything," Shirley fussed. "At least learn how to change the ink in the copy machine."

Basil preferred to assume that life would be as it always had been, perhaps a little more automated than before. He had weathered it in the past, and had actually advanced and outlasted most of the others who had been hired about the same time.

The full-length mirror in the hall reminded him of why the interns unfairly and unkindly dubbed him Ichabod Crane. It annoyed Basil to read Washington Irving's description of Crane as "tall, but exceedingly lank, with narrow shoulders, long arms and legs, hands that dangled a mile out of his sleeves, feet that might have served for shovels, and his whole frame most loosely hung together. His head was small, and flat at top, with huge ears, large green glassy eyes and a long snipe nose, so that it looked like a weather-cock perched upon his spindle neck, to tell which way the wind blew."

Yes, Basil was lanky, and his nose was obvious, but he was neat, his head was long and thin and his ears served their purpose without being conspicuous. There really wasn't a similarity.

He detested the modest maroon tie that Shirley had set out for him, and instead chose a navy tie with gold flecks.

He blocked Oscar Wilde's attempt to escape into the outside hall and quickly shut the door. It was a daily routine and he knew he should remember to shut the young fox-colored cat in the guest bathroom before he tried to head out. He walked down three flights to the street and to the bus stop half a block away and glanced at his watch.

A long line had gathered. Longer than usual. He might not get a seat. He might not even get on the bus that would get him to his job on time. *If I walk to the next block for the next bus, I might make it. Maybe the lines won't be long at the next stop. I could take a cab.* Shirley would have a Plan B. Possibly a Plan C. Another bus arrived, disgorged two passengers with shopping bags, then five commuters with briefcases squeezed on. Brakes squealed, taxis honked as the bus pulled through the red light. Basil checked his wind-up Bulova that had been his father's. The time hadn't changed since he had slipped it on his wrist while dressing. He shook his arm. The second hand moved slightly, started, then stopped. When had it stopped?

He reached in his pocket for his flip phone to check the time. It was gone, as was his wallet. Had he left them on the table in the hall when he tried to keep Oscar Wilde from escaping, or had the man who had bumped into him a minute ago extracted the contents of his pocket? There was no boarding any bus now.

It was too soon to panic. Basil took off at a lope, pushing past the jay-walkers at the intersection and dodged the wandering tourists looking for a breakfast spot. At first the pace was exhilarating, and he even smiled as he quickly covered two blocks. *I should do this more often,* he thought. Another block and he felt a twinge in his right knee and his lungs began to object. His leather-soled shoes were not meant for jogging on pavement. He stopped and leaned against an overflowing trash can. Seven blocks to go. Basil released his tie, wiped his brow with it, and shoved it in his right pocket. As he was about to start again, he felt a tug on his pants—the right pocket area had been snagged by a frayed wire that anchored the trash can to a lamppost. His step backwards released it, but left a navy flag of torn fabric hooked on the wire. His tie. Maybe Samantha has a sewing kit in her drawer. It wouldn't be her kit, because no one in her generation repaired anything. They just threw things out and bought something new. But maybe a repair kit was left there by Mrs. Joyce Royce. She had transferred three years ago after twenty-five years at the publishing house to the Ozzies' newest venture, timeshare management, in one of The Towers.

Basil's lungs burned. His shoulders were hot. His dress shirt was soaked. He reached for his tie. Only half of it was still in his pocket. The rest had slipped like a blue and gold-flecked snake through the hole and was now hanging halfway down his leg. A small urchin walking by grinned as Basil pulled the tie back into his pocket.

"Mister, will you teach me how to do that trick?" the boy asked.

Basil stuffed the tie in his left pocket, and ran on without responding. *I'm not a magician, dammit,* he thought.

Three blocks to go. He had lost sensation in his left foot; he gasped for air, not caring how polluted it might be. He hopped over dirty rugs spread with faux watches and cell phone covers, narrowly avoiding a vendor setting up a display of hunting knives.

Only one block left. He stopped, panting. He had to pull himself together. Basil studied his reflection in a cigar store window. His face was flushed, his eyes bulging; heart thumping. He resembled a drunken neighbor knocking at the wrong door at three A.M.

He smoothed his graying hair and straightened his jacket. If Samantha didn't have a repair kit, perhaps he could use a stapler to hold his pants together until after his meeting with the Ozzies. No time to waste. With slower strides more suitable to a professional man, the chief editor at a small but prestigious publishing firm, Basil reached the revolving door.

"Amanda?"

"Dad?"

The doors revolved a second time as they stared at each other in the lobby.

"What happened to you, poor dear?" she asked, her blue eyes studying him with concern.

"Long story. Well, short story, but I'm late for a meeting. What are you doing here?" He called over his shoulder as he raced to the elevator and pushed up. The doors opened and without waiting for her answer, Basil stepped inside and pushed No. 14. to Ozburn, Ozburn & Ozburn (Sangria's name was added just two years earlier). It occupied the entire thirteenth floor, which for superstitious reasons was renumbered the fourteenth when Sangria became a full partner.

The Ozzies were waiting in the conference room. Howard, the oldest sat at the end, Willard, two years younger sat to his left. Sangria, Willard's twin, younger by five minutes, was on Howard's right. Gretchen Peterson, from marketing, stood at the at the white board, and Evanna Manks, the "literary agent" (with vocal fry) was seated next to Howard—a pile of manuscripts in front of her. Next to her was Angel Romeo from acquisitions.

"Sorry I'm late," mumbled Basil.

"Twenty-one minutes and forty seconds, to be exact," said Sangria, heavily coated with cosmetics and swishing her dyed-brunette curls. She looked at her tablet. "And what happened to you? You look a bit of a mess."

"Uh, missed the bus," said Basil, trying to remember where he had stashed the tie.

The Ozzies exchanged glances. Basil knew from looking in the store reflection that some might think he had been rolled for his valuables after an all-night bender and had slept in an alley. He knew they really didn't want to know the details of his mess, except perhaps, Sangria.

Howard cleared his throat. "Basil, we know that your time is limited here—coming to an end—and you are winding down your official duties, but Evanna here has been asking about the *Bovine Royalties*, or whatever title for the book. How's it going? She says the author, Kenly Pope is going to be hot and we want to push this book into print. Big sales. Chick Lite. Romeo brought cover ideas from the art. Pope looks great on TV. Easy to book."

"If I may speak for a moment," interrupted Evanna. "I'm surprised we haven't heard from you on this one, Basil. Three of your staff members got back to me immediately and said thumbs up. You've had it since Tuesday, and not a single text. I'm dumbfounded by your lack of immediate positive response."

"I don't text, and I have only had it a week or so," said Basil. He didn't admit he hadn't looked at it until yesterday. The Ozzies' eyes were fixed on him. They all leaned forward. He tried to gather his thoughts but they were as stray as the feral cats behind his apartment building. Basil rubbed his hands together, and cleared his throat. "Yes, it has possibilities, but I like to read an entire manuscript before I pass judgment." His words were slow and deliberate, not designed to inflame or arouse conflict. The words of a calm and experienced manager.

"No first impressions? No gut instinct?" pressed Evanna in her cultivated voice. The Ozzies were sympathetic to the agent's questions.

"Actually, the title needs changing," Basil said.

Evanna spun her cell phone on the table's surface. The top ended up facing Sangria. *Not a good sign,* thought Basil. Sangria took this as a cue.

"Evanna is right. The title is perfect. That's what readers are looking for these days. Somebody's son or daughter or wife in the title. Makes them feel included, like someone might write about them or they will know someone in the book. We haven't had much gender diversity in this line, so the idea of a queen's son is quite attractive."

Basil's Adam's apple bobbed. He decided to politely stick to his position as he always had in the old days when publication conferences involved old man Ozburn, not his offspring. Basil allowed himself a moment of distraction. What about a title like: *The Founder's Sons and Daughter*. Or, *The Publisher's Incompetent Children*. How that might sell!

He gripped the table. The faces told him to reconsider. The art director held up a mock cover with Kenly Pope's title already in place.

"The title's very long, too long," Basil heard himself persist against his better judgment. "No one will be able to remember it long enough to place an order."

He felt he should stop talking but the silence, but the chilly silence, wouldn't let him. "You know, if readers can only remember the Queen's Son part, they might order something about Elizabeth and Phillip or George, instead of this book."

Evanna spun her jewel-encased phone case again, and again it pointed to Sangria.

"Basil, there is no choice here. Everyone loves the book and it will be an immediate best seller. Marketing will see to that. Get it done. Finish your editing. Kenly has a prequel coming, and a sequel. It's going to be big," Sangria responded. "It must be done and soon!"

"Okay," said Basil. "If I may be excused."

"We'll want an update every afternoon at five, beginning today," said Howard, "and copy Evanna on it too."

"Sure," said Basil. As he stood, he hastily covered the tear in his pants with his briefcase, and walked purposely from the room, down the hall into the editing room, past Samantha, who averted her gaze, and into his office where the grinning portrait of old man Ozburn, somewhat affectionately dubbed "Popgun" by his offspring, was again hanging upside down. Basil wished he had curtains on the windows that opened to his staff's area. When OMO was running the place, before the advent of gray or tan cubicles that blended with the latest décor, curtains would never have been needed. His staff would be respectful. They would be observant of who was coming and going in the chief editor's office, but would always be busy with their tasks. Now they could watch his every move by peering over their computer screens and plot mischief when he was away from his desk.

Basil righted the painting without looking through the glass windows at the staff. He kicked his shoes off his still-throbbing feet, stapled the tear in his pants into a ridge of torn fabric that looked like the Grand Tetons, and found his crumpled tie wadded in his left pocket. Shirley would press it without questions, he hoped.

He should call her to see if his wallet and phone were on the hall table, or in the bedroom, or in another pair of pants he planned to wear but had taken off when he noticed what looked to be a Jackson Pollock streak of spaghetti sauce. He dialed home. No answer. He wondered if he should leave a message, or just start calling banks and credit card companies to cancel everything. And what about the phone? Amanda would see this as the perfect opportunity to force him to use the smart phone. His head hurt. Was it from one too many glasses of port last night or one too few?

He called his home again, and this time left a message, trying not to sound frantic or concerned about his missing items. Shirley would come back from yoga, or shopping, or a visit with Amanda at HW&W's gluten-free juice bar, would look for the phone and wallet and would call back with reassuring news. Then he would walk home. Calmly. Serenely.

The door to the main editing room opened and Evanna walked in and stopped at the newest intern's desk. How does an agent get such access and influence? he wondered, unless, unless...

Why had things changed so dramatically at O.O.&O. since the Ozzies's had taken over? Even OMO would be surprised at how his children were disregarding the venerable traditions of the company and were running it as if it were just another business in their ever-expanding portfolio, including numerous mysterious and foreign connections.

Basil glanced furtively around his office to see if anything else needed righting before taking up his red pen for his morning's read of Kenly Pope's words.

Something still wasn't right, but he couldn't place it. Oh, the wastebasket, and his *Chicago Manual of Style*. Both upside down. If there was anything else amiss, it would have to wait. He avoided the actions of the warthogs. He glanced at his watch, forgetting that it was of no help without winding.

He turned to the page he had flagged with a sticky note, and began reading, crossing out cliches, and trite expressions that he detested, but were all the rage, such as "gone missing." Why not simply say, "was missing." The more he read, the more he crossed out. Kenly Pope's first few chapters were much better than subsequent ones. Sloppy, missing punctuation. Misspellings once in a while, such as "it's" for "its." He disliked the overused and meaningless "impossibly," as in "impossibly blue eyes." Shirley's eyes reminded him of cornflowers, but they weren't impossibly blue. Maybe Pope was just rushing through the writing without rereading.

Or Pope had a friend or family member edit it—someone who would offer praise rather than criticism. Why wouldn't agent Evanna send the manuscript back for improvement rather than push it on O.O.&O. and a rush job at that? This was going to take longer than he anticipated and his deadline for completion was a few weeks away.

There was a sharp knock on his door, and it opened before Basil could respond.

"Excuse the interruption," said a thirty-something young woman, with large rose-tinted glasses, spiky dark hair, a gray business suit and green high heels. "I'm Clarisse, from Clarisse."

"From who?" asked Basil, wishing he had said "from where."

"Clarisse. You haven't heard of Clarisse? We decorate all the big places now, including The Towers."

"This isn't a tower. And not a big place. If you look around, you can see it is simply my office, and I'm rather busy," Basil complained.

"Sangria called for me, honey. She said to take measures, and come up with a plan so we can make changes, dramatic ones—all the latest colors—next month for when you retire and your replacement arrives, *comprendez-vous*?"

Basil blinked. Yes, he had retained his favorite chair through several redecorating purges, and had resisted all efforts to repaint the beige walls or replace his heavy oak desk, but it hadn't occurred to him that his space would so quickly be edited (was that the right word?) when he retired.

"You don't mind, do you?" asked Clarisse, but it was not a question. She pulled a measuring tape from her large mauve-and teal-colored sack with O.O.&O. emblazoned on the side. She placed her clipboard on the corner of Basil's desk, precariously near the framed picture of himself, with Shirley, and Amanda at about age eight. Amanda was holding a small black cat that Shirley had named Sole because it was always underfoot. Amanda preferred Inky.

"I really am rather busy," said Basil as he moved the photo away from her clipboard.

"I won't be long, honey," said Clarisse. She pulled the metal tape out of the dispenser and stretched it across the door frame. "Three feet," she mused, writing it down, and letting the tape snap back inside its case.

Her heels clicked as she walked to the only wall with an outside window, although the view was of a fire escape and alley filled with trash, including a discarded Christmas tree that hadn't moved in three years.

"Basil," she said, "if I may call you that, can I bother you to give me a hand?" Again, it was less a question than something that was expected of him.

He wanted to insist more firmly that he was too busy, but it was clear that she knew that and it didn't matter. Besides, she had played the Sangria card. Sangria had sent her.

He sighed and rolled back his chair.

"Now stand over there and hold the end of this," Clarisse directed. "It will only take a few minutes."

He knew that wouldn't be the case. Clarisse slowly measured things that he wouldn't have thought of, including the oil painting of OMO. Basil wondered what would happen to it when he left. By Clarisse's measure, it was an impressive three by five, not easy to upend by pranksters. But about five years ago the Ozzies had added sets of hooks and hanging wires to the bottom and sides so that it could be done, though not without effort, as he so-well knew.

Amanda hated it even as a fourth grader. "Daddy, you should make them get rid of it. His smile is creepy." She was even more insistent as a teen after she met OMO and his children at office family picnics. But she and Sangria had immediately hit it off.

Basil agreed privately, but the old man liked its prominence in the editorial area (rather than in his office), and besides, his wife, Margarita, had painted it. She knew something about her husband's smile that eluded everyone else.

The old man, at least, knew the publishing business, hired knowledgeable employees, and had a proud list of titles on Ozburn House's front and back lists. He was often invited to major social events, including a party with Elsworthy, the former temporary Librarian of Commodities, several tipsy senators, and a dozen also tipsy and loud congressmen. The gathering was hosted by lobbyists, and that spring OMO was asked to speak at two high school commencements on why books should be read, not just used for decoration. It was a not-so-subtle plug for one of the company's new titles called *The Real Life of Books* that quickly rose to the top of the New York *Times* list.

In those days, prospective titles went through the traditional process, and like most houses, Ozburn (singular at the time) was known not for literary selections or biographies of national celebrities, but for books that would enhance the lives of readers, and make them think.

Occasionally, there might be a slim volume of poetry that was printed on elegant paper with deckle edges and with a gold ribbon sewn into the spine. Basil always suspected that sometimes the poet's pen name was one that Margarita had come up with for her own creative efforts, but it was not his to judge. Instead he would make spelling and capitalization suggestions. One can never get involved with telling poets what to do with such, or with rhyme or spacing. Poets have their own rules. Even reasonable editorial suggestions, such as corrections to capitalizations and punctuation, were often tossed by poetic waves to the shores of outright rejection.

Undaunted by quality, unashamed of banality, or the absurdity of writing about cocktail party humor, Margarita held book signings, sold her books to her friends and because she had small press runs, reprinted often and was able to boast on the verso page of the fifteenth reprinting in less than a year. When her friends and acquaintances declined to be pressured into filling their shelves with more of her verse, she had adopted a series of pen names, and Basil had heard through the interns that she appeared in disguise at her book-launch parties and signed copies with her other monikers. Her outfits and dialects were so outrageous that H. E. Minton, a columnist with the *Daily Observer*, could be counted on to attend just to write about the absurdity of it all. In a nice way, of course. He counted on free copies of new books to sell on his social media accounts.

As Basil walked the tape along the wall below the window to the editorial room, his phone rang. He moved quickly toward it.

"Dang, we'll have to start over," fumed Clarisse as he dropped the tape and it recoiled, snapping her hand.

"Shirley?" asked Basil.

"You Basil?" asked a deep voice.

"Yes, may I help you?" Usually Samantha screened calls, but there had been no buzz to alert him to the caller's identity or mission.

"Found your wallet," said the caller.

"Oh, thank heavens," said Basil.

"Empty," said the man, "except for your business card."

"Empty?"

"Empty. In a trash can near a bus stop."

"No credit cards? No cash? No driver's license?"

"Empty. You want it back?"

"Oh yes. Sure," said Basil. It had been a Father's Day gift from Amanda before she would have nothing to do with animal products. Her new employer was developing faux leather with a soy-oatmeal base. Early tests were not promising but crows liked the flavor (as the trash collector had reported after Christmas last year).

last of his generation. Several old-timers had taken an early retirement to travel or move nearer to grandchildren, three had retired for medical reasons. Then there was Barb Knolly, whom he admired for her kindness and memorization of the *Chicago Manual of Style.* She had dropped dead at her desk one Thursday afternoon at age sixty-five. Howard Ozburn II gave a touching eulogy before the EMTs arrived (they were late because they had been looking for the thirteenth floor), and told everyone they could have a thirty-minute break with pay. Fortunately her funeral was on a Saturday so that no one had to take time off work to attend. Barb would have understood.

Age didn't matter—at least no one seemed to talk about it. Basil had been hired out of college (his father was an acquaintance of OMO), and willingly started at the bottom—the first floor, and worked his way up through the various departments.

Like the others at the time, he was glad to be employed and to learn all aspects of the business while waiting to be noticed and promoted. In the after hours, or even during lunch, there were great discussions of literature, artists, musicians and authors. The conversations were stimulated by Ozburn House's initial location in the artsy section of the city where cafés leaked folk music and smoke into the streets. Later, before the advent of electronic books and devices, and a generation more attracted to video games than the printed word, OMO moved the offices to a modest skyscraper (thirteen stories) in the Tower District. A dwarf among tall buildings, OMO told Basil that he wanted the big guys to think he was looking up to them, when in fact they would be coming to him to have their stories published. He had connections. With his connections, he could guarantee them spots on national television—all the morning shows. He would go after the celebrity, tell-all market as his niche. And he did. Rare was the new fiction, which was why Basil had been surprised to have the Kenly Pope manuscript arrive on his desk so late in his tenure.

Basil thought that O.O.&O. should stick to the wretched tell-all books by celebrities and politicians, of which there was a growing number, and seemingly endless talk shows looking for guests. Interviewers didn't read the books, except for those on public television and radio. Instead, the publisher's publicity department, would develop a list of questions—the more controversial the better—and a few inflammatory quotes from the book. Either the celeb author or the interviewer would hold up the book jacket to face the cameras, at least five times so the readers would have time to jot down the title.

As soon as the celeb left the studio, the book would be tossed on a lunch room table for station staffers to take home. Some sold the free books on line, noting that they cost more because they were autographed. Reviewers did the same.

Not likely to happen with Kenly Pope's book. Terrible title and fiction. Basil picked up where he left off. Ash wasn't making any effort to help Dresden. Apparently she knew the identity of his mysterious attacker, which meant she had seen the person's face. Basil guessed, based on the author's sympathy for Dresden, that the writer was male. Who else would name a dog "Grunt?"

Another tap on the glass door, and it opened before Basil could respond.

"Excuse me," said a thin man with a short sandy ponytail pulled from hair on the top of his head. He pushed his glasses up his nose. "Don't mean to bother you but Sangria wanted me to have a look. Do you mind?" The name tag hanging from a lanyard indicated his name was Marco Jones and the logo under it appeared to show he was from Clarisse.

Marco carried two large books of color swatches, fabric and paper. He looked around but saw no place to set them down except on Basil's desk.

Basil realized he hadn't said a word, but couldn't think of anything to say about this new intrusion. Sangria again.

He moved Kenly Pope's manuscript a foot to the right so that Marco could work with his color books.

"You're a great help," said Marco. "Maybe you'd like to assist. Sangria wants to change the colors in all offices. Each department will have a theme, and I'm assigned yours, though I realize you won't reap much of the benefit of this new era." He cleared his throat. Hearing no response from Basil, he continued. "Anyway, have a look."

"These are all primary colors," said Basil. "Rather bright."

"I knew you'd get it. I told them you should be consulted," said Marco, beaming.

"Red is all about the body. Blue affects the mind. Yellow, well that radiates self-confidence, and green reflects both mind and emotion. Now, orange, my preference, represents endurance creativity and enthusiasm." He studied Basil's impassive face.

"What do you think?"

Basil couldn't think. How could anyone work if the walls were painted any of these bright colors. "You would dilute them, wouldn't you?"

"Oh, no!" said Marco. "The point is to modernize and have staff work at peak creativity. My question is should we go with one color per work area, or a combination for maximum effect?"

"Stripes," said Basil, hoping his sarcasm would be noted. It wasn't.

"Fabulous idea!" said Marco. "I love it."

"Window shades. Curtains. Borders," Basil said peevishly.

"Perfect. See what a little creative yellow on your desk will do?" He pointed to the swatch. "Wait till I tell Sangria!" Marco whistled as he scooped up his sample albums. He hummed as he smiled broadly at Basil.

A few of the interns had finally drifted back to their workstations, late as usual, but were seemingly occupied. Basil realized that it was mid-afternoon.

Still no call from Shirley, and no further communication from the phone voice. The powdery crackers had worn off, as had his hunger pangs. A new sensation had taken hold—a combination of fear and worry. He'd better call his banks to report his credit cards as stolen. He had no idea of the numbers on them nor how to reach the emergency customer service desk. That was printed in tiny type on the back of the plastic. He would ask Samantha. She would know how to get that information for him. He could count on her discretion, he hoped.

Her extension was busy. He tried again and her voice mail said that she was away from her desk. "Leave a message." He wouldn't. He dialed home again. His answering machine, with his voice: "Leave a message after the beep."

Maybe he should contact the police. They would know what to do and how to contact the banks. He knew they had a non-emergency number, but what was it? He tried Samantha again. This time her message indicated that she was gone for the day. Some sort of family problem.

"Damn!" he complained, slamming his phone. Samantha should have told me she was leaving. An intern? Surely an intern would know how to get this information for me. They're high-tech.

He stood and looked through the glass window. Darwin. Pale Darwin. Darwin's doughy face needed ten minutes under the broiler to look healthy. Basil straightened his tie and tried to relax. He didn't want to appear to be as inept as he felt. I'll ask Darwin.

Darwin, one of the older ones, was hunched over his computer, spinning a small red object between his thumbs. It looked dangerous. Basil decided to use caution in approaching him. He cleared his throat loudly. When that didn't work, he tapped Darwin on the shoulder hoping that wasn't against boss-employee harassment regulations. Darwin jumped, dropping the spinning object into his lap then deliberately blocked his computer screen with his shoulder as he swiveled around.

"Yes, sir," he said. "How can I help you, sir." Darwin's eyes reminded Basil of when he had caught Amanda at age seven lying about brushing the cat's teeth. A combination of guilt and glee. A stubborn but refutable denial based on bubbles foaming from Inky's mouth.

"I'm wondering if you could assist me with something personal," began Basil.

"Of course, sir," replied the intern. "Give me a sec to shut down." Basil caught a glimpse of feminine underwear as the screen dimmed. *Likely a present for his mother,* he thought.

The little spinning thing quickly disappeared as well.

"Darwin, I need help finding the non-emergency number for the police station, and also the consumer help numbers for my banks. Bank of America, Capital One, Capital Two and Third Fourth Bank, and maybe something else."

"Sure," said the intern, with apparent relief. Darwin typed the queries into his search engine, and printed the results.

"Here you are, sir. Anything else? Are you having computer problems?"

"Just issues," said Basil. "Much obliged. Thank you. Sorry to interrupt your work." He rushed back to his office before the spinner reappeared and Darwin resumed his surfing.

"You in trouble for porn?" asked Aquelle from the next cubicle.

"Nah, the old man just has issues," said Darwin.

Basil noticed his message light was blinking. He pushed PLAY. It was Shirley. "What is going on, sweetie? You've called home six times. I've had calls from your bank. Something about credit cards maxed out, and Oscar Wilde has been puking hairballs all over the house. Do you want salmon or swordfish for supper?"

Credit cards maxed out. The thief hasn't wasted anytime. He's probably on the way to Switzerland or Panama to open a bank account.

He looked at the papers that Darwin had printed for him. I'd better call the police first, then the banks, then Shirley.

Basil was relieved that the customer service people actually provided customer service. He was told that his cards would be replaced in a few weeks after they investigated and the thief's charges removed from his account.

He called home. No answer. He left a message. "Shirl, I'll be a little late and salmon will be fine."

He chose not to discuss the hairballs. He was sure they would be there and he would probably step on at least one concealed in the design of the oriental carpet in the hall. It was Oscar Wilde's favorite depository.

His phone rang. It was Sangria. "Checking in, Basil. Be at my office at five to go over the manuscript's progress. Don't knock. It will disturb Cleopatra. She's had a stressful day."

He couldn't remember if Cleopatra was the new intern, the one with large glasses in a green frame. Or was she the temp help, who had been hired to work in receivables? He had bumped into her near the break room. She had been a little too friendly.

Basil glanced at the wall clock, gathered up the papers that he had barely had time to work on, adjusted the remnants of his tie, and headed to Sangria's office. He might not make it to the rendezvous with the caller. Perhaps that would be the end of it.

3

Cleopatra had been Amanda's idea—a service comfort chicken to help calm Sangria's nerves. It was difficult for her to be the third partner at O.O.&O., especially when the other two were her brothers.

Pets are known to be therapeutic, but Amanda knew that Sangria didn't like hamsters, was terrified of all dogs bigger than a teacup Yorkie, and she abhorred tropical fish after her brother Willard's friend, Phil, had flushed her goldfish, Ethel, (deceased for more than a week). She feigned tears, but in truth, she hadn't fed it.

Over their just-girls' mid-morning snack two days earlier at Tofu-Aria, a vegan café that featured opera, Amanda had suggested a hen. A rescue hen, the Cuckoo Marans variety, that had been saved from the slaughter house. Amanda had read about its escape from a poultry truck near the municipal park named for the controversial Confederate Private Bubba Beaufort. When the hen was captured, the public, spurred to action through social media, demanded that she be freed. Total freedom was not the best idea in the big city, but the Poultry Rescue Society agreed to save the black hen and rehome her as long as her new companions didn't name her Bubba Beaufort after the park.

Amanda was stirred by the hen's story and promptly contacted the group. She couldn't keep the chicken in her new apartment, and knew that her parents would decline, so she approached Sangria with the plan. As soon as Sangria peeked in the soft carrying cage that Amanda had concealed under her chair, she was thrilled.

"A service chicken. How perfect," she cooed. "How does this work? I never had a whole chicken, just breast."

"Cleopatra will cluck soothingly during the day in your office," said Amanda, hoping that would be the case.

"You will enjoy stroking her feathers. It's sort of like the comfort and elegance of a feathered boa. Occasionally she might lay an egg. A chocolate brown egg."

"Organic?" asked Sangria, reaching her pointer finger through the netting to stroke the hen's feathers.

"Organic and gluten-free," said Amanda. "You'll be able to sell eggs to the interns."

"If they look like chocolate, they'll be great for Easter," said Sangria. She was clearly smitten with the possibilities. She knew in her professional network this would cause clucks of approval and probably many copycats. She might even be written up in *Publishers Weekly* and other trade journals. She envisioned herself on a *New Yorker* cover. She'd be on the Today Show, but toyed with the idea of accepting Fox New's offer first. A hen in the Fox house. She smiled at her own cleverness.

"Now we must think of a name," she said, reaching through the mesh to stroke the hen's wing. She ignored the sudden peck. "Give her time to know me," said Sangria.

"Definitely a name that references a strong woman," said Amanda, thoughtfully. "Nothing silly like Biddy or Henny-Penny."

"Juliet?" suggested Sangria.

"No, too romantic and besides, Juliet died. We don't want this chick to be thinking death, at least not yet."

"Josephine? One of the queens? Bathsheba?"

"Hmm. Not quite the right image," said Amanda. "How about Cleopatra?"

"I like it," said Sangria. "Bold, beautiful and tough. We'll make quite a pair."

With that decided Sangria had more practical questions, such as what to feed her service chicken. "Don't they eat bugs and worms?" asked Sangria. "I read that in one of my picture books."

"Yours will be a vegan, dear," said Amanda. "It's much better and besides Cleopatra will not be outside roaming around a dirty farmyard with other animals. She will be living in a pure environment in your office. We can get the interns to build a little pen and house for her. Some fake turf to give her the feel of the outdoors, and they can make a perch for her to sit on your windowsill and look at the sky and the street while remembering her happy childhood."

Sangria sipped her rosé wine and smiled thoughtfully. "This is the best present I have ever been given. It will help me relax. Is it true you can teach a chicken to play the piano? I saw one do it on the Internet."

"You just never know what a chicken can be taught," replied Amanda. She looked at her watch. "Hate to eat and run after just three hours, but I've got errands. I assume you can handle things with Cleopatra. There's a little bag of starter chow in the pocket of her carry case."

"Stop by the office," said Sangria, "when the interns are done with the construction."

Amanda failed to mention her plans for Sangria's service chicken to her father during dinner that night. It didn't seem like something you could casually drop into conversation when Basil was so worked up about politics, not just national ones, but those in the office. She preferred not to engage in it either when he had already let his gold tie drag through the organic mashed vegetable soup. She watched him then wipe the tie on the tablecloth, a dull green streak. He was worked up, but silently. Both Amanda and Shirley knew from his facial expressions, the rise and fall of his eyebrows, the bobbing of his Adam's apple, that his head was full of nightly heated arguments—mainly of things he had wanted to say to the Os and the interns. So Amanda decided to wait a day or so before she brought up the hen. There was no point either in talking about the future with him in a such a mood.

She and her mother had been privately discussing a special trip after Basil's retirement. Shirley agreed to gather information on possibilities. She thought about when she and Basil first dated. He was tall and thin, had more hair, and smiled. Conversation was easy and fun, wasn't it? But in recent years, with the dress codes for senior employees, then for just him, when the other senior employees were replaced by the interns, he became agitated. Soon everything seemed to upset him. She had wondered if he could last until retirement. His nerves were frayed. He became forgetful. Poor dear. Shirley was glad she had Amanda to talk and shop with. Amanda had suggested that Shirley and Basil take a cruise or a getaway somewhere after he retired. It would be good for both of them to get out of the city and not focus on his old job. Shirley thought that was a lovely idea and the two of them made an appointment with a travel agency geared to recent retirees. Shirley filled a brown folder with brochures and warned the agency not to send her e-mail or catalogues. She wanted the trip to be a surprise for Basil.

As Basil prepared to knock on Sangria's door at five, as she demanded, he noticed that the glass window in her door was covered with newspaper. He heard pounding.

Sangria called, "Come in," and then, with her back to him as the door opened, she said, "Put the straw over there."

Three interns were adding finishing touches to what looked like a chicken coop. Basil briefly wondered if it was a prop for a photo shoot for a new book Sangria was planning to launch.

Then she swiveled around and he saw what she was holding, no cuddling, a black speckled hen. Oh, I thought you were from the feed store," she said breezily. "Have a seat."

Basil edged closer to her desk, trying not to step on chicken wire and boards. His head throbbed with questions that could find no voice.

Sangria placed the chicken on her desk, and scattered seed over a bright yellow binder.

"Cleopatra," she said. "My comfort chicken. She's already calming my nerves." She stroked the hen's shiny feathers.

"Amanda gave her to me. A lovely, thoughtful gift." Sangria studied Basil's face, looking for a reaction. She could find none.

He tried to clear his throat but couldn't. It was closing. He held back a rising sneeze. As a child he was allergic to his feather pillow. It was replaced with a foam one. Maybe Cleopatra could be exchanged for a rubber chicken.

Sangria watched him grope for a handkerchief, watched him dab his watery eyes, watched him clutch his throat.

"I know everyone will come to love Cleopatra," she chirped. "Listen to her cluck. It's so soothing. We will all be more productive now that we can have stress-free offices. I've sent a memo to the interns that if they feel that a service animal will help them, have at it."

Basil wondered if there were allergy pills in an intern's desk. No, this was beyond over-the-counter solutions. He would need to see an allergy specialist after work.

"Basil, I've forgotten why you made this appointment," said Sangria.

"You asked *me* during the morning meeting," Basil choked out. "You said you had a question."

"I've got to get back to work," said Sangria. "By tomorrow I'll be getting calls from major news outlets. They'll want interviews and pictures. This is big business news. Maybe I'll write a book or two."

She picked up Cleopatra and carried her to the window. "Isn't this better than being on that dirty street, sweetie pie," she said, nuzzling the hen's feathery neck.

Basil slipped out. He couldn't go to the allergist. His credit cards had been canceled. He needed to see the stranger about his wallet. He had only a few minutes to reach the arranged location in front of Pizza and Sprouts. He knew he wouldn't make it. There was no point in running. No point at all. By the time he reached Pizza and Sprouts, the evening commute had filled the streets and sidewalks. He was jostled but enjoyed grim satisfaction that there was nothing in his pockets to pick. He stopped briefly, wondering if the thief, the stranger, had come or gone or was one of the customers imbibing in trash-can pizza that was hairy with green growing things. The empty wallet no longer mattered. He glanced around. He saw no one he recognized from the morning. He heard no gruff voice at the crowded bus stop.

Basil continued, pushing like a breast-stroke swimmer until he reached his block. Only a few more doors and he'd be able to go up to the third floor and remove his painful shoes and have a double port with Shirley.

"Hard day?" asked Alto, the doorman. He looked Basil over carefully. "Maybe you should clean up before the missus sees you. Frankly, you look terrible."

Basil mumbled a thanks, but headed straight in and up the stairs. He reached for his key. His pocket, the one with a hole, was empty. Basil had no choice but to push the buzzer.

"Who is it?" An eye stared out the peephole.

"Me," said Basil, uncertain of who was on the other side. He heard the chain slide and the door opened. It was Amanda.

"It's Dad," he said, sneezing.

"Oh my gosh," she said, opening the door wide. "Daddy, I didn't recognize you. Oh dear, what happened? Have you been eating red meat again?"

Basil gave her a quick peck on the cheek. "Let me get cleaned up a bit," he said. He wanted to see if he looked as bad as he felt. He wanted to throw away his trousers before Shirley could see their condition.

"It's after six but we still can have a happy hour," said Amanda, "and you can tell me all about your day."

He closed the door to the bedroom, slipped out of his torn trousers, wadded them up along with his tie and hid them in the back of his walk-in closet. Basil rummaged for a pair of his old maroon sweatpants and a cammo shirt that Amanda had given him for a "someday" camping trip. She called them comfort clothes. He could only find navy fleece pajamas with cartoon pink flamingos printed on them. Another gift. He needed comfort. If his paternal grandmother, bless her soul, were still alive, she'd make him milk toast topped with a dollop of real butter and a sprinkle of salt for supper. Maybe he could talk Shirley into fixing it. But the household toast didn't have gluten, and Amanda would quash the idea of milk and butter.

"Focus," he said to himself. His mother said that a lot.

Basil felt a little blubbery. It had to be the allergy to the hen. He ran a comb through his thinning hair, and headed for the kitchen where his daughter and the glass of port awaited.

"Where's your mother?" he asked after the first warming sip.

"Late," said Amanda. "She left a note. Some man had called about finding your wallet, and she was supposed to meet him somewhere."

"Oh no!" gasped Basil, stifling a sneeze. "You didn't try to stop her?"

"I didn't see her. It was just a note. I just got here myself, just a few minutes before you. I'm sure she'll be all right. She's been packing Polly Pistol, you know." Amanda extended her hand with her pointer finger aimed ominously. "Don't worry. She'll be fine. Those lessons at the shooting range paid off."

"I've got to find her," said Basil. "She could be in danger." He placed his unfinished libation on the table and jumped to his feet.

"You can't go out barefooted," Amanda called, but her father had already barreled out the front door, shouting "damn cat." She hoped he hadn't inadvertently found the hairball that she heard Oscar Wilde deposit while her father was changing in the bedroom.

Basil first noticed his lack of footwear when he reached the cold sidewalk. He walked briskly, neck down, hopping from one side of the walk to another, ignoring the stares of passersby as he dodged dog deposits, gum, and sticky trails of spilled sodas. How many blocks to Pizza and Sprouts? he wondered. A cop blew a whistle warning jaywalkers they could be ticketed.

With feet sore and cold, Basil arrived at Pizza and Sprouts. It was closed. A scrawled handwritten sign in the window said *Family Emergency*. Basil pounded on the locked door, hoping that someone might be cleaning up. Mopping. Washing dishes. Harvesting sprouts. Anything.

Maybe Shirley and the stranger were out back, or meeting in an alley. He rushed around the block until he found the alley behind the restaurant. His better judgment kicked in. You can't go there with bare feet, and you shouldn't even go there with shoes. Focus. Deep breaths.

"SHIRLEY! he bellowed. "SHIRLEY!"

"Mister, can you spare a five?"

Basil spun around. He wondered if the voice was familiar. No the stranger with the wallet wouldn't be asking for just five dollars. He'd want more for the wallet's return.

"I have nothing," said Basil, trying to gain his composure. He pulled the pockets of his pajamas inside out to prove it.

The panhandler, about the age of the interns, stared in disbelief at the tall wild-looking man in flamingo pajamas.

"You don't even have shoes. I gotta place you can stay the night if you bring your own cardboard."

"Thanks," said Basil. "That's very . . . uh, very kind. Actually I'm looking for my wife. Maybe you've seen her. She's about this tall, dyed red hair (he wasn't sure; she changed color every month) and she is looking for a man with a leather wallet. Real leather."

The panhandler seemed to be deep in thought. "If you don't have a cardboard blanket, I could probably find you one. There's a soup kitchen run by the nuns two blocks away. More than soup some days. We could make the line if we hurry," he said. "You look like you could use a hot meal."

Basil thanked the man. "I really need to find my wife. She might be in danger."

"Okay, buddy, good luck," said the panhandler as he trudged off.

Basil wished he had something to give the poor fellow. He normally didn't carry change in his pajama pockets. Not that it mattered. He had nothing to put in them.

A hand tapped his shoulder. He turned and saw a cop. "I'd like you to come with me, mister," said the officer, not unkindly.

"I haven't done anything, sir," said Basil, cautiously. "I'm just looking for my wife."

"Your eyes are rather bloodshot. Are you sure you haven't had a nip too many?" The officer studied Basil's face.

"A chicken," said Basil.

"Hmm," said the officer. "A chicken. That's a new one. But beers all have funny names these days. So, what's your name and address, pal?" the officer asked. He appeared to be about to write something down, while mumbling into a shoulder microphone.

"Basil Randall Beale Jr."

The officer said, "B-A-Y-Z-U-L . . ."

"No, no," said Basil. "B as in Basil, like the herb, A as in, um, Alphabet, S as in, um, Stamp, I as in Ibid., L as in Lede."

The officer looked puzzled. He crossed out what he had written on his pad. "Wait a minute. You mean, B as in Basin, A as in Asian, Z as in an herb that I never ate."

"No," said Basil, gritting his teeth. "B as in Barcelona, A as in Arctic, Z as in Zoo."

"I thought there was no Z in Basil," said the officer. "I think you need to come with me. You look cold, sir. I can drop you off at a nice warm shelter where they have soup."

"I've got to find my wife. She might be kidnapped."

"I'll file a missing person's report," said the officer. You can spell her name for me after I check you in to the shelter. He took Basil's arm. "Let's go, fella."

"I just want to go home!" Basil shouted, "SHIRLEY!"

To his surprise, he heard, "There he is! Over here, dear."

Shirley wasn't in the alley but in a cab that had pulled up to the curb behind him. She hopped out.

"Basil, sweetie, what has happened?" He felt her warm arms wrap around him. He hung his head on her shoulder.

The officer asked, "You know him, ma'am."

"Yes," she said, looking over Basil.

"Will you be safe with him?"

"Oh, yes. He's a gentle man. Just wandered a bit tonight." The cop didn't look convinced.

"Come, dear," she coaxed Basil.

He followed and slumped in the backseat of the cab. He wished he had his slippers. Anything to warm his feet.

"Here's your wallet," said Shirley as the cab lurched forward in time to stop at a red light.

It was empty, just as Basil feared. "How did you get it?" he asked hoarsely.

"We'll talk over dinner," said Shirley. "You look terrible. I think a steamy shower and comfy clothes will do you a world of good. I will call Amanda's vitamin coach."

"Not Dr. Nasturtium, or whatever his name is," said Basil. "I'll be fine. I just need a blanket."

"Whatever were you doing in that rough neighborhood without shoes or a coat? You could have been mugged. Or were you mugged, dear?"

"This morning. We'll sort of. Someone bumped me and stole my wallet and credit cards."

Shirley didn't seem to be listening.

"Amanda said you acted strangely all day at the office. The interns were concerned enough to tell Sangria. She had to spend extra time in pet therapy to calm herself after your meeting, and of course, Sangria was concerned enough to call Amanda."

"Everything was fine today," said Basil through a clenched jaw. "As fine as it could be considering . . ."

"Here's our building, you can pull over," Shirley told the cabbie. Basil opened his wallet to get a tip for the driver, then realized the foolishness of that gesture.

Basil followed her to the building's entrance where Alto opened the door and said, "Found him?"

"I'm fine. Just fine. Everything is fine," said Basil as they headed to the elevator.

Shirley rummaged for the door key in her large red handbag. Basil pushed the buzzer, and within seconds his dear daughter, thoughtful Amanda, had wrapped a fuzzy blanket around his shoulders and handed him his unfinished glass of port. "Oh, Daddy, we've been so worried. You didn't answer your phone. Just look at you."

She steered him to the hall mirror with its frame covered with seashells. It looked out of place in the front hall filled with Victorian furniture from Shirley's side of the family. But Amanda had made it in Scout camp, Camp Cocina Largo, when she was eleven. He didn't recognize his face. His eyes had a wild depressed look that reminded him of Oscar Wilde when he was about to fire off a hairball. He dropped his gaze. He had seen enough.

Amanda said gently, "Now have a sip and I'll pour some more."

"He needs a bath," said Shirley from the kitchen.

"Shower. Bed," responded Basil.

"Supper will be ready in ten," said Shirley.

Basil shuffled to the bedroom and shut the door.

When Amanda heard the shower running, she quietly opened the door and laid out clean pajamas and slippers, then left the room.

"Mom," she said, "Should we call for help? He may have amnesia or a breakdown. Do you suppose he's on drugs? I hear that the people closest to addicts are the last to know sometimes."

"Let's see how he does after a good meal," said Shirley. "Your dishes should make him happy."

Amanda's meal did not make him happy, but the third glass of dry port did. Shirley and Amanda chatted across the table to each other, darting occasional looks in his direction. Basil chose to eat in silence. What was there to say? He hoped that the subject of what had happened would not come up, but of course it would. Shirley began, "So, sweetie, it's important for us to know about the events of the day. It was obviously not one of your best."

Basil struggled. Where could he begin? There was no point in going into details except about his wallet, and credit cards being stolen. So that's what he told them. He had been pickpocketed.

"But, love, you kept calling and some stranger kept calling and Sangria kept calling," said Shirley.

"Things happen in the streets," said Basil, sipping his port. His explanation sounded good enough to him that he repeated it.

Shirley arched her eyebrows in the direction of Amanda. "I think you should eat the rest of your special meal, stay home and rest tomorrow," she said to Basil.

"Can't," said Basil. "I must finish editing a novel and meet with the hen. If you excuse me, I'll take my wallet and go to bed." He looked on the hall table where he thought he had placed it. "Gone again," he said in a voice that teetered on a wail.

"No," said Amanda. "I threw it out. It was leather and quite falling apart. I'll get you a new one. Cork is all the rage these days."

She gave him a hug. He was too tired to complain. In her embrace he noticed a tiny black feather caught in her sweater. His eyes itched again.

Damn chicken.

4

Basil didn't finish Amanda's signature dish of tofu pork, quinoa salad, organic baby spinach dressed in pea milk ranch-style dressing. He had stared at the dark crunchy things sprinkled on top and not so politely pushed the salad aside when his beloved daughter mentioned what sounded like "crickets." He excused himself and went to bed, despite Shirley's entreaties that he needed more sustenance. He had considered sending out for a bacon-sausage-cheese pizza but closed his eyes instead, hoping that the events of the day were simply a bad dream. He didn't hear Shirley quietly open the bedroom door, cover his feet, and grab a nightie so that she could sleep in the guest bedroom. She closed the blinds and the heavy curtains so the sun wouldn't wake him, placed a cool hand on his sweaty brow, and whispered, "Poor dear."

It was nine A.M. when he heard the scratching on the bedroom door. Oscar Wilde could not be deterred any longer. The cat wanted in so he could sleep on Basil's pillow—his daily routine.

The room was still dark. Basil rolled to his left and squinted at the digital display on his alarm clock. Disbelief, then panic. He was already late—a third day, and the Ozzies would have his head.

Frenzied, he dressed, not caring if anything matched, and dashed past Oscar, who bolted between his legs for the unmade bed.

Shirley was sipping watermelon tea in the breakfast nook, her second cup. She liked to catch the bubbles that the tea made when it was poured and make a wish. The more cups, the more wishes.

"Basil, dear, do you feel well enough to be up today?" she asked.

"Late. Late," he said. "Call a cab."

"I think Amanda already told them you're out sick," said Shirley.

"Can't," said Basil. He couldn't think beyond single word responses. His head hurt, and the thought of seeing Cleopatra again made his nose itch in the direction of a sneeze.

"If you insist," said Shirley, "but given all you've been through . . . By the way, the mustard tie doesn't go with your green jacket. Not the right shades. Sangria can be rather critical, you know."

Basil teetered on apparel uncertainty. "I don't really care," he finally mumbled.

Shirley looked startled. "That's not nice, nor like you," she said. "Change your tie. No, I'll get one for you, while you eat that piece of toast."

"Not if it's gluten free," said Basil, more boldly than was his comfort zone.

"Please try to calm down and get back into your right head," said Shirley. "You can't go off to work with that attitude."

Basil knew she was right. He wouldn't last the day with the Ozzies, let alone the few weeks left. His fingers selected a dense dark muffin of unknown genetics, and his mouth opened obligingly. But unable to swallow the bite, he took a sip of Shirley's tea, and was sorry.

Shirley returned with a pale yellow tie with little green books printed on it. A Christmas gift from the Ozzies several years ago.

"Tuck in your shirttails, put on shoes and socks and I'll make you a sandwich for lunch. Something healthy, dear."

Alto had talked the cabbie into waiting for Basil without doubling the fare. Basil gave him the address and tried to fit Shirley's lunch bag in his jacket pocket. It didn't fit. He placed it under the seat. Focus. Focus. He closed his eyes, then realized that the cab wasn't moving. The meter ticked, however.

"Can you step on it?" Basil asked. "I mean, I'm already late."

"Look, buddy, we're not moving until that crowd gets out of the way. They're picketing one of The Towers today."

"Can't we take a side street?"

"They're everywhere. Don't you read the news?"

Basil vaguely remembered something about a demonstration but the cause escaped him

"Maybe I should go on foot," he ventured.

"Your choice, buddy," said the cabbie, "but if I were you, which I'm not, and frankly I'm glad of that because you look like hell in those colors, I'd call in sick or just telework. Then you don't need to wear that tie. Worse yet, you need a haircut."

Basil leaned to the right so he could get a better look at the man behind the wheel. He didn't resemble the stereotypical cab driver. With graying red hair and a reddish beard, he looked more like Mac McGregor, his former barber, who had disappeared about ten years ago during the middle of a shave. Something on the cable television news that played in the shop had upset him. Mac had yelled, "You stinking bastards," and stomped out. With his foamy razor.

Basil would have found this mildly interesting—something to talk about with Mrs. Joyce Royce later during a coffee break, except that he was the one in Mac's chair. Half a shave. Half lathered. He had to wait twenty minutes for one of the other barbers to have time to finish the job.

"Mac?" he said. "Mac the Barber?"

The cabbie swiveled around. "I knew it was you, Basil. I recognized that stupid tie. Howya been, buddy?"

Basil wondered if he should ask, but decided since Mac might still be prone to unpredictable behavior, that he shouldn't initiate that line of questioning. But he found himself rubbing his chin, wishing for one of Mac's expert shaves.

"Been fine, Mac. Getting close to retirement, not that I want to leave the firm just yet," Basil said.

"They pushing you out?"

"Feels that way. But you know, lots of young people looking for jobs and willing to work cheaply."

Mac honked impatiently. Traffic was at a standstill and demonstrators were pushing between vehicles in the direction of The Towers. Basil tried to make out their signs. He sighed. There were almost weekly political demonstrations at The Towers. One thing or another.

The meter was still running. Basil saw that he already owed $20, which was all the cash he had.

"I'd better walk," he said, handing the bill to Mac. Basil opened the door, bumping into a demonstrator, who made a threatening gesture, then took a picture of the cab's license plate.

"What about the tip?" complained Mac as Basil closed the door. "A tip's customary, you know."

The crowd was even less forgiving than Mac. Basil thought he had seen his former barber raise his fist in his direction and was relieved that it did not contain a razor.

Alto was watching from the front door, waiting to see if Basil would return to his apartment, or head off on foot. Basil was having the same thoughts. If he returned home, he could call the office and tell them that he was ill, something Shirley or Amanda had already done. Or he could brave the demonstration.

But Alto blocked him at the door. "Excuse me, Mr. Beale, anything wrong?"

"The cab isn't moving, and I don't think I feel well."

"Mac can take you to the doctor," said Alto, gazing at the taxi that hadn't moved.

"No, I'd rather walk, I mean, I should call my office."

"Here's my phone," said Alto. "You call and I'll go tell Mac to wait."

Basil stared at the cell phone. His mind had drained. He couldn't remember anyone's number. He placed Alto's phone on the doorstep and dashed in the opposite direction, away from Mac, Alto, and the demonstrators.

He had no idea what time it was.

Maybe he could hitch a ride. That could be dangerous, even though he had seen it work in the movies. He'd look for a vehicle that looked safe. The truck of a baker or florist. A butcher might be carrying knives. He jaywalked after a block and turned to the left, went three blocks and turned to the right so that he was headed back in the direction of O.O.&O., hopefully out of the range of the demonstrators. They should have reached The Towers by now.

Traffic had stopped again, an angry combination of successive red lights, double-parked delivery trucks, scooters swerving, and line painting.

Warthogs and Feathers

Basil saw an opportunity. He stuck out his thumb in the direction of the driver of Cable TV 13: "Your Eyes for News." The van stopped and the driver said, much to Basil's surprise, "Hop in the back."

He wasn't the only passenger. In the seat behind the driver were Teri Ecki, who did regular features on the nightly news, and camera woman, Missy Blomberg, whose name scrolled in the credits. Basil was giddy with his good fortune.

People he knew, well, felt like he knew.

"Where you headed?" asked Teri, as she applied rouge.

"O.O.&O."

"Now isn't that a coincidence! So are we!" said Missy.

"Are you there for the big story?" asked Teri, blotting her nose. "We thought we had an exclusive."

"No, I'm the senior editor. What story?"

"We don't want to leak it," said Missy. "Really huge."

"If he works there, it's probably okay," said Teri. "But don't say a word until after six."

"You have my word," said Basil, pleased to be in their confidence.

"Sangria called us," said Teri, "about her new therapy chicken, Cleopatra. I bet you are just as excited about the publicity for the firm."

The women weren't sure how to interpret the silence and a choking sound from the back seat.

He finally said, "Your secret is safe with me."

The driver noting the steady heavy volume of traffic asked Basil if he could recommend a good place to park for a couple of hours. Basil offered his own space in the underground garage.

"I never use it," he said. He escorted the TV crew to Sangria's office. It might make up for his late arrival, and his plan worked. Sangria's face melted from hostile to extravagantly welcoming as he ushered in Teri and Missy, and Steve, the driver, who was carrying their camera gear.

Basil asked to be excused and hurried to his office, where the interns quickly slid into their cubicles when they saw him. Their heads were down in concentration, their fingers busy at the keyboards.

Samantha's desk was still empty and tidy. Sticky notes—mostly phone calls that needed to be returned—adorned his door. Basil was relieved that no one had asked for explanations. He righted the upside down pictures and items on his bookshelves. Two new ceramic warthogs had been arranged in embarrassing postures. That would never do.

He loosened his tie, picked up his red pen and continued to read *The Devine Royalty Social Club Queen's Son*. It wasn't improving. The best chapters were still in the beginning. The author seemed to have lost his train of thought, and had even changed character's names, without consistency. Grunt the dog, by chapter 15, was called Iota, and Dresden was Dalton or Dryden. *Sloppy. Basic editing or proofreading should have caught this.*

5

"I hope he wasn't too much of an annoyance," Sangria said to Teri.

"Who?" asked the news reporter.

"Basil. Our chief editor. He's retiring soon—age-related, but don't quote me," she said.

Teri checked her makeup making sure that a small blemish to the side of her nose, where she had squeezed a blackhead, was adequately covered.

"Basil was fine. He was hitchhiking, which we thought was sort of cute, for someone like him, and then he let us use his parking space."

Sangria's eyebrows arched, then furrowed. She made a couple of notations on her new sticky pads with a tiny chicken logo printed in the lower right corner. She needed to move the interview along; another station would be arriving in an hour or so.

"Where would you like me to sit?" Sangria asked.

Teri snapped her compact closed and looked around. "Where's the chicken?"

Sangria smiled and walked over to the coop that she had shrouded with a black cloth for dramatic effect. "Voila!" she exclaimed, flipping the cloth off the cage. The motion terrified Cleo, who flapped frantically while leaving white gooey droppings on the formerly pristine straw.

"Oh, my! Is she dangerous?" asked Missy, backing up the tripod.

"Absolutely not. This is only her first full day on the job. You can see how ruffled I am about this interview—our debut. But watch how Cleopatra will calm me when I have her in my arms." With that, Sangria unlatched the cage's door and reached for the black speckled hen. Cleo eyed her warily and pecked Sangria's hand, drawing a drop of blood. Sangria suppressed her desire to shriek, fearing that the interview might immediately end badly.

Instead she made clucking sounds and sang a lullaby that she vaguely remembered her mother, her nanny or someone singing to her. She heard the click of the cameras rolling. Good stuff, she hoped.

Cleo relaxed as Sangria cuddled and stroked her. "We're calm, aren't we, Teri?" she said. "You can see how calm I am with my therapy chicken. I am calm when I answer the phone, or see an e-mail from an intern, or go to a stressful board meeting. Would you like to see me be calm at a meeting?"

"Yes," said Teri. "Tell us first how holding the chicken—and I know this is no ordinary chicken from your press release—makes you feel."

Sangria closed her eyes in contemplation of the perfect answer. "Before I had this chicken, I was always stressed. Stressed. STRESSED. But when she's in my arms, I'm calm. I feel her little heart beating faster than mine. I know I must be calm for her. But, really, it's all in the feathers."

"Feathers?" asked Teri, taking notes although it was all being captured on tape.

"Feathers," said Sangria, with new authority in her voice. She stroked Cleopatra. "They are soft and shiny. Not like a cat's fur or dog hair. You can try holding her at the meeting—a stressful meeting—I plan to meet with my staff later. You'll see what I mean."

Teri looked skeptical. She knew all about the stress of meetings, and she secretly dealt with hers by trying to remember all her Facebook friends while her boss rambled on at staff meetings that had nothing to do with the day's news. She had cultivated a slight smile and appeared to be attentive. It didn't always have the proper effect. The station had brought in an expert, a doctor (not medical) Melicia Martina, to discuss sexual harassment. Melicia, as she wished to be called, interrupted her monologue to ask what Teri thought was so amusing. Fortunately before Teri could respond, there was a large thump. Alfred Daltry, a cameraman and known womanizer, had fallen asleep. While he was being revived, Teri shifted her expression to be "earnest and attentive."

Teri wondered briefly if O.O.&O. had had similar seminars for employees. Or any seminars on any workplace issues?

Her station manager called staff in for such meetings at least once a week, regardless of what breaking news they were working on. It was compulsory, and rarely seemed relevant, at least now that she was one of the most veteran employees after thirteen months on the job. Plus she had already won a READY, an in-house trophy for always being immediately ready to gather her pad, pen, makeup, and her crew to get to the scene of the action.

And the assistant station manager told her privately that Teri had a real nose for public interest stories. That was just a week ago. And that's why Teri was ready for the opportunity to get the scoop on the service chicken.

She would have to play it straight. She could not make Sangria look foolish in the eyes of the millions of viewers. She needed to ask more questions and have more shots of Sangria and Cleopatra interacting. Maybe someone could enter the office and provide stress. Yes, that would show the viewers how the process would work. "Show, Not Tell," was one of her station's mottos, though not particularly original.

"Sangria," Teri interrupted, "Let's set up a scene where something happens to cause you stress, and you could explain how did the former stress manifest itself, and how does this chicken calm you down."

"Hmm," said Sangria thoughtfully. She tilted her head back and closed her eyes while tickling Cleopatra's wattle. "I used to chew my nails. And, I'm afraid to admit it, but I also sucked on my thumb. Just the knuckle, not the whole thumb, mind you. In just one day my nails have grown back, thanks to Cleo," Sangria said, proffering her fingertips for closer examination. Teri signaled the cameraman for a close up.

"As for a stress demo, um. I know. We'll summon Basil and ask him how his editing is going for our new book. Yes, that'll do it. I will be stressed." Sangria used her intercom to page Basil to her office. "Pronto!"

Within five minutes he opened the office door a crack and said, "You called?" His nose twitched in anticipation of feathers.

"Please come in," said Sangria, while the cameras rolled again. "I need a status report on Kenly Pope's book." Her face morphed into a stressed expression. Her eyes widened and with a trembling hand, she dabbed her brow as if to remove unflattering perspiration seeping through her makeup.

Basil stepped inside, but only a few inches. He surveyed the crew from the TV station and the camera now trained on him. His throat began to close and his eyes watered. He croaked, "My allergies," before he sneezed, so loudly that Cleopatra flew out of Sangria's arms and landed on the top of a bookcase.

Basil was unable to stifle a second explosive sneeze so he took advantage of Sangria's efforts to coax the bird off the shelf and left her office, quietly closing the door.

The scene was perfect for the six o'clock news—the local interest segment. Sangria had clearly looked stressed by both her employee and the hen's ability to fly to new heights. When Cleo was back in her arms Sangria once again had a relaxed smile. "See," she said. "It works."

Teri realized this could be a big moment in her career, not so much the chicken as a profile of Sangria, once of the up-and-coming names in the publishing world and social scene. She'd pitch it once she returned to the office. But there were a few more questions to ask.

"So, will you be adding other chickens or a rooster in the near future?"

Sangria's head was buried in Cleo's silky back. It sounded like she replied something about a nest egg.

"Cut," said Teri. She signaled to the crew to leave quietly.

"One station down," said Sangria, when the door behind them had closed. "The other networks will be here soon."

Basil returned to his desk, ignoring the inquiring looks from the interns.

He turned to page 40 of Kenly's book. Had he already read this part? Perhaps. He skipped ahead to page 50, then 80. There was the end of his red marks. The author had brought Ash back into the story line and she was in court, handcuffed, a first appearance for disorderly conduct. She had been part of a demonstration against closing the local tattoo parlor. She had soaped the windows of the adjacent children's clothing store that had recently opened, when the owner complained to city officials that the nasty tattoos that were unfit for children to see.

Basil circled the entire passage and crossed it out. "Stupid," he wrote, not caring what Sangria thought.

He couldn't imagine wanting a tattoo, and was dismayed when eight years earlier, before Amanda became an almost vegan, she had come home with a small tattoo on her ankle. Even under close examination, Basil had not been able to tell if the ink depicted a swan or a giraffe. Amanda laughed and said, "Oh, Daddy, it doesn't matter. Big Ben is just a beginner and I was doing him a favor. I was his first customer, and he only charged me five dollars."

"You paid for this? It's a tattoo typo," said Basil.

"Call it what you will, but Big Ben's a friend from high school, and when he gets more confident he'll be doing piercings."

"Absolutely not on you," said Basil. "He'll have to answer to me."

"Don't be so old-fashioned, Dad. I won't let him do my nose or tongue."

Basil decided not to say anything more about the piercings. He was afraid to ask where else the rings might go.

"Just wear socks until the tattoo washes off," he said.

There were a lot of other things he had never considered doing. Spiky hair gel, a guayabera shirt, a pedicure, or a personal trainer. Climbing Mt. Everest. Owning a gerbil. And never a therapy pet nor would he ever hold one for the owner ever again.

Basil shuddered as he recalled staying in a shabby motel after his car had broken down in a New England town with just cheap motels. On the second morning while he awaited the only repair shop to get around to replacing the water pump, he was having so-called breakfast in the tiny room where there was a coffee pot, a toaster, a pitcher of unidentifiable yellowish juice, muffins wrapped in waxed paper imprinted with blue dots, and generic cereal.

Missing having his morning newspaper, he read glossy brochures about local tourist spots and carefully placed them back on the rack.

As he sipped his thin black coffee, he became aware of a woman in a fuzzy yellow bathrobe standing next to him. "Here," she said, placing a small, fluffy tan dog in his lap. The dog was wearing a little jacket that said COMFORT DOG.

"I'll be right back," the woman said.

"Wait," said Basil, but she was gone. The dog stared at Basil, and he thought he detected a snarl.

"You can't have a dog in here, mister," said a tall man, holding a drooling toddler in his arms. "This is an eating area. No pets."

"It's a comfort dog," responded Basil.

"Let me see your papers," the man said.

"I don't have them, you see . . ."

"Here, watch Misty while I find the desk clerk." The man plopped the toddler on the table next to Basil's plate. She quickly grabbed his muffin and fed a piece to the dog. And then another, as Basil watched helplessly.

The dog's owner returned, her damp hair in curlers. She smelled of lavender and nutmeg.

"What?" she shrieked. "You let your child feed my comfort dog? Didn't you read on the instructions on his jacket? Don't touch, don't feed. Comfort dog in training."

Yes, Basil remembered the encounter well, and also the lecture he received from the desk clerk for not notifying the motel that he had brought a dog with him.

And then there was the Service Iguana on the flight he had taken from the city to Tampa. It was large and took up most of his seatmate's lap. And the cat that a woman had hidden under her long skirt. She had ordered at Martini when the flight took off at nine A.M. Basil, of course, had asked for water. The woman soon asked Basil for his water so she could give some to her cat. He obliged, wishing that he had had the fortitude to say no.

He regretted that he had been such a nice guy all his life, and rarely even thought of wishing he had courage.

Now he wished he had the guts to trash the warthogs and walk out, leaving behind the damn Kenly Pope manuscript, and unread sticky notes. So what if he didn't get a bonus at retirement, or had a black mark on his career, a nasty post on social media by the Ozzies. So what if Shirley shook her head and said, "You were so close and you blew it." So what if Amanda choked on her sprouts. He would be free.

He glanced at the wall clock. It was already two P.M. Three hours until he would need to report to Sangria. Perhaps he could suggest a neutral location, such as the board room. Away from the damn chicken.

Shirley knew better than to ask about his day when Basil kicked off his shoes in the front hall, then mumbled curses at Oscar Wilde. The poor cat couldn't help himself. The new hairball potion from Dr. Larry wasn't working. Shirley knew she ought to check the front hall carpet every afternoon before Basil's arrival, but she had been busy going through travel brochures with Amanda. When Basil arrived forty-five minutes earlier than expected, Shirley gathered up the papers quickly and secreted them in the china cupboard beneath her mother's Irish tea set. Fortunately Basil immediately headed for the bedroom to shower and change without realizing Amanda was in the house.

Shirley and Amanda were making progress on the surprise travel plans, eliminating the latest spots on the travel advisory lists, which covered an increasingly large portion of the world. Egypt, long a place Basil had talked about, was iffy, as were many places in the Middle East, Venezuela, inland Colombia, parts of Mexico, a neighborhood in Boston, train stations in France, and most airports. Shirley wasn't sure about visiting most places in the United States either, so the thought had crossed her mind, to have a big retirement travel costume party at a house in the country, hire a caterer to prepare foods from many nations and watch travel videos. Perhaps representatives of cruise lines and travel books, like Rick Steves, could be enticed to join them. Amanda said that although the idea was "cute," her dad would not like to wear a costume, especially if someone took pictures on their smart phone and posted them on social media, and then Basil and everyone at the party would be instantly criticized for being politically insensitive about other cultures. It could ruin him and smear his name.

Shirley responded with horror. "I never thought of that. Poor Basil, after all these years of having a unblemished career, it would be terrible for him."

"And us," said Amanda, thoughtfully. "And the Ozzies."

"Let's have another look at what the agent suggested," Shirley said.

"How about a cruise?" asked Amanda.

"He gets a bit queasy sometimes," said Shirley.

"Then fly to one of those all-inclusive resorts," said Amanda. "They are supposed to be safe for tourists. You never need to leave the walls of the compound. And they treat you like royalty."

"Hmm," replied her mother. "I'd like that, but Basil doesn't like a fuss."

"How about a Dude Ranch? Or some other adventure, like mountain climbing, or white water rafting. Or learning to herd sheep or raise sustainable crops. Dad used to like adventures."

"That might be good for him. A real change of scenery and pace. Something to make him feel young again, but I'd prefer to sleep in a comfortable bed. No outhouses."

"Hey, I have an even better idea, Mom. You used to talk about a little lost girl that I thought was only a fictional character, but later you said that she was Dad's first child, Mora, and that she had disappeared from his life because of her evil mother. Well, lately I was wondering about her and decided to search online, and guess what? I found her," said Amanda. She looked at her mother. "And she has been looking for us."

Shirley said, "You did? Why didn't you tell us?"

"I was going to, but Dad's been so preoccupied, the moment hasn't been right. Anyway I know where she is, in the Cook Islands doing research on something environmental like snails. What if I reach out to her and invite her to his surprise retirement party? Just the family."

Shirley looked at the ceiling for a moment, then said, "Do it, but maybe she should come here first so we can get to know her a bit. He's out of the shower so you'd better slip out quickly."

"I'll do some research," whispered Amanda. "Mora could even help with the plans. See you tomorrow," Amanda said. She tiptoed out.

Shirley handed Basil a small glass of port after he tossed his socks in the laundry after shaking them out over the kitchen trash container.

She poured a chilled Pino Grigio for herself and followed him into the living room where he settled into his recliner. Oscar Wilde jumped to the side table and studied Basil's lap.

"Darling," said Shirley, "I'm worried about you. You just haven't been yourself lately." She pulled up a footstool and rubbed Basil's feet. "Anything I can do? I was out all day so I have a special dinner for you tonight." He longed for meatloaf and mashed potatoes and real butter, not another batch of tofu and soy. He'd even settle for a TV dinner. Her face didn't offer a clue to the surprise.

Basil sighed. He wanted to tell her that he felt increasingly useless in a job that he had loved. That he felt old and was being pushed out. That he was surrounded by juvenile nincompoops and equally nincompoopy adults who were running things. But that wasn't a nice thing to say, and if you couldn't say anything nice, you shouldn't say it at all. That's what his mother would tell him. Shirley would be shocked at his increasing despair. She would tell him to relax, to take it easy. To go with the flow. To not let things get you down. To count to ten. And she'd tell Amanda, who would stress the importance of veganism to have a balance in his life. For health and happiness to never place meat on his plate again. And could he dare mention how much he hated live chickens? No, Amanda and Shirley would both have something bright and cheery to say about Cleo, the comfort hen. Well, maybe, just maybe, he should get himself a service wolf! That should take care of that darn (no, damn) feathered creature making his last few days with the Ozzies increasing miserable.

Shirley's massage felt good and so did the warmth of the port. He downed the rest just in time to avoid Oscar Wilde's leap to his lap, which brushed the hand holding the glass. Oscar's increasingly heavy body, his tawny and russet coat, and black ears settled into a purring extravaganza. Basil sighed again, and closed his eyes. Shirley extracted the glass and took it to the bar to refill when Basil awoke. Supper would wait.

Refreshed from a hearty TV dinner of meatloaf, lots of real butter for his brussels sprouts, plus gravy on his mashed potatoes and real bread, that had been buried in the freezer, plus an undisturbed night of sleep, Basil was ready to "seize the day." That was what his father always commanded, although usually in Latin—*carpe diem*. His father stressed that how each day went was based on attitude. Think positively, and your day would be positive. (Father had been reading a book on the power of positive thinking, and quickly became a believer, dragging everyone else with him.) But what if it worked? Basil didn't know because his father had never shared his office days with the family. Father read the paper on the train, had a bourbon or two, and mowed the lawn or puttered until dinner was served. If the day had been seized, Basil never knew. But, yet, it might be worth a try if the Romans had felt it was important.

"Carpe diem," Basil said as he entered the lobby the next morning and pushed the button to his floor.

"Carpe diem," he said to the substitute receptionist.

"The carpet needs cleaning? I'll take care of it," she said, adjusting the Hello My Name Is badge provided by HR. Basil didn't notice that her name was Edwina.

"Carpe diem," he said to the interns.

"Sure. I'll get the copies made soon, sir," said Babs, the newest one. "Just checking my e-mail."

"Carpe diem," said Basil to himself as he pulled the sticky notes off his door frame, and righted the warthogs, separating three that had been arranged in a new unmentionable pose. "No more ménage à trois, my little porcelain and hairy beasts."

He was feeling better. He made a flower on his desk out of the sticky notes, fanning them out around his coaster. "Carpe diem, little notes." His new attitude was exhilarating.

"Carpe diem, Kenly Pope," he said opening the manuscript. He had forty-five minutes until the morning staff meeting. He would be positive and ready. He would arrive on time, buttoning the two lowest buttons on his suit coat as he walked through the door just like television attorneys do. He would not be surprised nor dismayed by whatever Sangria said or did. No, he was still the editor-in-chief, still the senior department head. His opinions mattered, and he would share them if the subject of Pope's book came up. He would be objective with his reading, although, that also meant having his red pen at the ready. It was.

He turned to page 135. A flashback. Ash and Dayton were sitting on the a creek bank shortly after his narrow escape from the abandoned social hall. She had been released on her own recognizance. His small dog, Grunt, panted and drooled under a gum tree. They were unconvincingly reminiscing about their junior high school teachers, although Dresden could not shake his fears about what had happened in the social hall. What had that evil person been doing in there? What did it have to do with MaMa and Aunt Poli?

Basil finished the short section and wrote, "Makes no sense. Cut."

The next few pages weren't much better. Suddenly Ash began rubbing Dresden's neck, and they became in a much-too-graphic tryst. *Well, at least they are seizing the day,* mused Basil. *But it doesn't resonate. They didn't even like each other a couple of chapters ago.*

Empowered by a sense of calm and positivity, Basil glanced at the interns' area. They had smiles on their faces. Bigger smiles than usual, as if they were all sharing in a funny joke. *It must be one of those social media things,* thought Basil. It looked like they were snickering or giggling as they shared whatever it was to each other's computers.

I will not be concerned that they are not working, thought Basil, smiling broadly. *Life is too short not to enjoy the moment. Carpe diem. Besides, it might be a funny typo that someone discovered.*

It was time to head to the upstairs conference room. He gathered the manuscript, a red pen and yellow pad. He unbuttoned his jacket so he could rebutton it at the appropriate moment and strode through the door, past the interns who were desperately trying to control their hilarity.

"Carpe diem, folks," said Basil with a friendly wave.

From the stairs Basil could see that the conference room was dark. Empty. Yet, the clock indicated that it was ten A.M. He heard the elevator door open behind him. Edwina came rushing down the hall. Mr.

Beale, Mr. Beale. Please forgive me. I forgot to tell you that the meeting location was changed to Sangria's office. I wrote it on a sticky note but it got stuck to my elbow, and I just saw it."

"Sangria's office?"

"Yes, on the fourteenth floor and down the hall to the right."

"I know where it is," said Basil, more sharply than he intended, especially on a day of positivity, which was now collapsing like a sandcastle hit by a wave. He darted into the men's room to get paper towels to take with him for his nose. The dispenser was empty. Toilet paper would have to do, but someone was in the only stall. Basil wanted to ask whomever to pass some sheets under the door, but thought better of it. He was already late for the meeting.

He burst into Sangria's office. "I didn't get the message," he stammered. His eyes immediately watered and his nose itched.

"We've been waiting for you, again," said Sangria. She sighed as she stroked Cleopatra. "But I want all of you to see something that you probably missed at eleven. Roll it."

Intern Murray pushed the play button on a computer that was set up to project images on a large screen set up behind Sangria.

Holding the hen wiggling hen, Sangria wheeled her chair to one side so that she could watch both the screen, and the staff's faces, but mostly Basil's.

"Good evening, I'm Teri with a wonderful story for you tonight. It's inspirational and could well be the new solution for stress management."

Basil rubbed his itchy eyes in disbelief. The segment, filmed just yesterday in Sangria's office, of course featured Sangria and the hen. Then, the camera turned and there he was, bumbling and sneezing his way into the office. No laugh track was needed.

"We're famous," said Sangria. She looked at Basil. "All of us. You were perfect in your role of stress-promoter. The interns loved it. I'll need you to come through the door again when channel WOOF 34 shows up later. No one could do it better. They are bringing a nurse with them to take my blood pressure upon your entry, then again after I stroke my service hen."

Basil found himself backing toward the door. "Can't." He offered no explanation. "Can't." He couldn't stop a succession of sneezes.

"At least sneeze into your arm," said Sangria. "WOOF will be here at noon."

Basil had no intention of repeating his television debut. Instead he called the emergency allergy clinic, and then a cab. Basil told Edwina that he wasn't sure when he would return.

The cab seemed vaguely familiar. The driver, definitely. Stocky, curly formerly red hair but graying.

"You don't look so good," said Mac.

"Allergies," said Basil. He covered his face with soothing wet paper towels from a different rest room on his way out.

"Figured," said Mac, "when you gave me that address. Watcha allergic to? The pollution hasn't been so bad lately."

"Chicken."

"I never eat chicken. Just steak or pasta. Don't want to get bird flu. I can drop you off at my uncle Rudy's eatery. No chicken on the menu."

"Feathers," said Basil. "Chicken feathers."

"That's a new one," said Mac. "My father always said, 'Horse feathers' when he was pissed. Which will it be lunch, or the sneezing doctor?"

"Doctor," said Basil, although he was feeling better.

"I'll wait, then we can do lunch."

Do lunch with Mac, with the meter running? He could tell Sangria that he had been kidnapped by a cabbie. Chicken feathers. Carpe diem.

Basil waited for twenty minutes to talk to the receptionist, then remembered that he couldn't be seen without proof of insurance and identification. He realized then that he didn't have a credit card with which to pay Mac, or cash to buy lunch. He wondered if he should slip out the back exit. Instead, he decided to try to take charge of his day and tell Mac the truth.

"No problem," said the former barber, with a hard glint in his eye. "You can owe me. I got a tab for people like you. Hop in."

Mac still had the same unpredictable voice. He was prone to shout a word in the middle of a sentence. In a book, an author would have put the word in all caps in the middle of a sentence. His single-word shouts startled his customers in the chair who were worried what he was doing with his razor. It amused others waiting for their shaves.

Rudy's Grille was thirty minutes away, across the river and through the suburbs to a small strip mall that had seen better days. The eatery was unpretentious. Paneling was halfway up the walls in a large open room. Basil noticed booths that needed refurbishing or replacing and small tables, with wadded paper under the legs to prevent rocking, were set in the middle. Had there been much of a lunch crowd, it would have been difficult to hold a conversation, but Basil and Mac were the only customers. Rudy, aside from doing the cooking, also waited and bussed the tables. As they entered, Basil had noted a HELP WANTED sign with a lengthy list of employment opportunities. Rudy later explained that it was hard to get dependable help anymore. Basil knew from experience.

As Mac and Basil surveyed the stained and sticky plastic-coated menus, Rudy suggested the daily special. Chicken tenders served with chicken soup.

"I thought you said . . ."

Mac kicked him under the table.

"I'll have the soup," said Basil.

"I'll see if there's any left," said Rudy. He returned from the kitchen with the bad news. "We're out."

"What else IS there, Rudy?" asked Mac.

"Peanut butter. And you can make your own sandwich. That saves on cleanup," said Rudy. "I'm expecting a big lunchtime rush. I only have crunchy today."

Basil liked smooth, but Mac replied enthusiastically, "Sounds good. Does it come with anything?" he asked.

"Give me a minute and I'll run to the store. Grape okay?"

It wasn't Basil's favorite; he actually liked a peanut butter and mayo sandwich, but he didn't want trouble. He studied the glasses of water that Rudy had placed in front of them and used one of the paper towels in his pocket to wipe what looked like lipstick off the rim.

"Some PLACE he's got here," said Mac, admiring the faded photographs of Las Vegas show girls taped on the wall,

Basil hoped a response wasn't expected.

"We're really proud of him. Our family's thinking of having Thanksgiving here, but we may make it a potluck and bring our own plasticware so he doesn't have to do so much."

Rudy returned with a small jar of jelly, dusted off the lid, and soon provided a half loaf of bread, two plastic knives and paper plates that he examined then brushed off.

"Bonz app-e-titty," he said, doffing his chef's hat before he returned to the kitchen.

"Carpe diem," responded Basil.

"Do what? Are we allowed to say that?" asked Mac.

"Never mind," said Basil. "Let's eat."

Shirley usually made his lunches, and rarely something as ordinary as peanut butter, which he happened to love. As a child he scooped it out of the jar and savored large spoonfuls. He experimented with sandwich spreads from marshmallow goo to chocolate pudding. His brother liked his peanut butter sandwich mashed with over-ripe banana. Shirley thought all of that was disgusting and Amanda said it wasn't healthy. She convinced her mother to fix Basil gluten-free bread with avocado topped with watercrest.

Rudy, on the other hand, had the right idea. Keep the menu simple. One item. And make it comfort food. That was exactly what Basil needed at the moment. Comfort, and Rudy's flagship food.

Mac was making a second sandwich. "You don't mind if this goes on your TAB, as well?" he asked

"Not at all." Basil was starting to feel optimistic, positive, and generous. He would buy a giant jar of peanut butter to keep in his office desk. He would affix a note to his glass door warning that his office was a peanut butter zone. He bit deeply into the thick sandwich, not minding that a sweet sticky red substance dripped onto his blue shirt. One sandwich would not be enough.

Mac continued thoughtfully. "You know, Baz, I was worried ABOUT you. But now you seems like your old self. Remember the time you tried to grow a beard? And once, a mustache? I liked trimming your whiskers. There was something special about them. Very unpredictable."

Amanda had liked his facial hair, but Shirley detested it. She said it made him look like he had had a nasty encounter with a pair of squirrels. At her strong urging, Basil gave in before the office party that year.

The party. Shirley had said something recently about the Ozzies' invitation to dinner. It was soon. Basil had told her that he didn't really want to go, but she had given him a look, and printed it in ink in the calendar.

"We must, dear," she had added. "I'll have Oscar's hair cleaned off your black suit."

6

"Where to?" asked Mac, slipping behind the wheel with a purposeful fart. In the barbershop, Basil would have winced when he heard Mac belch, and had been offended on a number of occasions by the ensuing, silent, passing of gas. Now, he welcomed this, and tried to emulate both from the cab's backseat. It would take practice, he realized.

"Show me around," Basil said. "I think I'll take the afternoon off."

Mac glanced back at him through the mirror. "Glad to, BUDDY, but are you sure you're okay?"

"Carpe diem," said Basil.

"Carpe what? I don't know that neighborhood," said Mac.

"Anywhere," said Basil. He stretched out his legs and smiled as he thought of Sangria pacing with the damned hen. She would be waiting for him to return, and expected, at the very least, an update at five. He didn't care if Kenly Pope, himself, or even the pope, were waiting for him.

What could the Ozzies do? Fire him? Well, he'd just file an age-discrimination suit or complain about animal harassment, and collect his pension. The interns would back him up. The TV station that had a made tape of Sangria's torment of him would prove it.

"Mind if I turn on the RADIO?" asked Mac.

"Whatever."

Basil used to correct Amanda and her friends when they responded that way. Now it was liberating. He went further. "Like, whatever." Like was another word that demanded correction. And "ya know, like, whatever." Now he felt free from the conventions of correctness.

Mac fiddled with the dial until Basil became concerned that he wasn't keeping his eyes on the road. He considered saying something, but remembered that Mac might still have a concealed barber tool.

It felt good to be bad. Basil had always been a perfect child, a parent and teacher pleaser. His grades were excellent. He practiced for his piano lessons. He made his bed and did the dishes when it was his turn. He cleaned the bird cage, even when it was his sister's turn, out of respect for the feelings of their parakeets, Bucky and Milly. "They don't like a dirty cage," he told his sister, quite often.

"So?" Beth responded with a yawn. She always hid in the bathroom just when their mother called them to a complete a chore. She knew that no one could challenge her reasons for being there. But every evening after dinner? Just when it was her night to do the dishes?

Basil was accepted at four Ivy League schools, settling on Princeton, where he had a triple major: English Literature, English English, and Piano Optics. It was rigorous curriculum, but had served him well in life.

Despite his height and frequent requests from the athletics department that he at least try out for basketball, Basil had declined. He had instead taken physical education courses that had the least impact on his body, such as Brisk Walking. He excelled at Brisk Walking, and hummed his piano compositions during this exercise.

He had always been the perfect employee. Neat, never tardy, polite and appropriately dressed.

For a short time he had a perfect marriage. He admired the talented dark-haired women with somber, smoky eyes. They married and had a brief honeymoon in Newark before both had to return to their careers. His in publishing, hers in art. He had met Margo at an art museum where she had a show of her metal sculptures, fashioned from of kitchen utensils. She continued working on new pieces, even after Mora was born. The baby was a bit of an interference in Margo's studio time, but she found someone to take care of her while she pounded and hammered the abstract sculptures, out of pots and pacifiers. Then Margo was accepted for her tenth gallery show. Basil wasn't really impressed. All he could say about the pieces that they weren't rusty. He had no idea what they were supposed to represent. At the gallery opening, a white tie affair, a critic studied one twisted and bent piece, titled, "Marriage," then muttered, "Awful." Basil nodded in agreement. Margo saw it all and with a smile, smacked Basil's face. Even though others standing around laughed, Basil realized that Margo was seething.

He had thought things were going well despite her complaints about his long nights at the office. But after the gallery show her premarital good nature changed and she was unpredictable and angry, even at his music. She began tossing her sculptures at the recycle bin. He fancied she was having a pre-midlife crisis or artistic stress.

He and Margo remained civil during their divorce discussions until she grabbed a crowbar, part of one of her sculptures, and ripped the keyboard out of his piano and hurled it out the window. She screamed, "To the fire pits of Hades, damned sonatas!" She wasn't referring to Bach, but to the ones that Basil had composed. Basil had heard a little gasp. Their dark-haired child, with big brown eyes, was clutching her stuffed alpaca in the living room doorway, a witness to the keyboard horror and her mother's newest rage.

No, he had done his best to be civil because of their daughter. He did not raise his voice even though he knew that would make Margo very happy. After Margo moved out with Mora, he simply had the locks changed, and called a thrift shop that accepted anything to come get the gutted instrument. When he hadn't heard from Margo in months, he bought an electric keyboard at a yard sale and continued composing.

He had always been decent, and that was the problem. As Amanda had observed, he needed to stand up for himself. She had taken business courses that counseled on how to ask for a raise or a promotion. He had listened and calmly responded that he didn't need a promotion because he was the head of the department, and his salary had been capped for years so there was no point in asking for a raise.

"You have a point," Amanda responded, with her winning smile. He knew her life course would be different.

He wondered what had happened to little Mora. Margo had made contact with her impossible. She had moved to the area because her geography professor thought so highly of the place. It was difficult to find reliable delivery service by Sherpas, and so Basil decided to wait patiently for when Mora, with so much musical talent even at age four, would reappear in his life. Basil fleetingly hoped each New Year's day that this would be the year that nasty Margo fall to some mountain disaster.

Mac continued surfing the stations, settling briefly on rap, then pausing to listen to "Nessum Dorma" on NPR, before choosing a rousing Calypso tune. He turned off the station quickly in disgust when it turned out it was a religious one with a preacher interrupting the catchy piece with a fire-and-brimstone message.

"Ever been to the zoo?" Mac asked.

"Not recently," said Basil.

"I used to take my boys. I always got STYLING ideas when I looked at the shaggy beasts. We especially liked the Highland Cow and the Valais Blacknose sheep. Boy, I could give them a great new look! Ever seen a yak?"

"Not lately," said Basil.

"Let's do it," suggested Mac, sounding a bit too enthusiastic. "I've got some barber tools. You could help me."

Basil was suddenly alarmed. "I don't think they'd like you to mess with the animals," he said.

"HAIR grows back," said Mac, making a sharp left.

Basil's brow dampened with sweat. He imagined the worse. He would be on the news again, but this time in an orange jumpsuit as he was fingerprinted for aiding and abetting. Mac would probably plead insanity, but Basil would have to explain and he couldn't think of an explanation. He would need to hire an attorney, but had no credit cards and no phone. Maybe the zoo would be closed. He couldn't check his watch; it had stopped working again.

Mac honked and swerved and cruised through yellow lights. Basil slouched so that his face could not be seen by other motorists.

When the cab stopped, he peered out. It was the zoo's parking lot.

"C'mon," said Mac, yanking open the back door. "We're here. We'll put the admission on your tab. I carry my own pellets."

Mac clasped Basil's shoulder. "My boys and I always started with the monkeys. The big apes. Frankie spit and hurled things. Sometimes PISSED at people. Good aim."

"You let your kids do that to people?" Basil blurted.

Mac gave him a look. "Youz crazy. Frankie was a fifty-five-year-old chimp, not my boy. My age. I think he recognized me. Just messing with us."

Mac paid the admission, but before putting the receipts in his wallet, he marked them with Basil's name. Then he handed a cloth bag with a drawstring to Basil. "Put this in your pocket. Look casual. I don't want to arouse suspicion in case someone recognizes me. You know, a lot of people know Mac the Barber. I've got our tickets."

The cloth bag clanked as Basil nervously slid it into his front pocket. What if he had to go through security and was caught with dangerous instruments? There was no time to worry or brood. Mac was moving quickly as he passed the guard and motioned Basil to follow.

"This way," he said. Basil's university skill in speed-walking training paid off. He was able to keep up with Mac who had the zoo layout memorized.

The yaks, three of them, were grazing in the back of the large pen that badly replicated their native land. They were not interested in Mac's whistled noises and outstretched palm containing oatmeal-colored pellets.

"Damn," said Mac. "Robbery. The ZOO'S make money by tricking tourists into buying this food crap, but then the staff feeds the animals something else that fills them up so it's a big rip-off. I make my own and bring it. Can I trust you, Baz? I add a little weed. Animals love it. What do you think, buddy?" Basil was about to agree, but the barber-cum-cabbie had moved on, dodging strollers, teens taking selfies with the elephants, and uncontrolled cotton candy and balloons.

When they reached the Valais Blacknose sheep housed with the Highland Cow, Mac stopped and crossed himself.

"Look at them," he said, eyes glistening. "Look at these FACES, the hair, the beards. Beauties. Wonders of creation. If God had had the time He would have been a barber."

Basil studied the hairy or woolly animals. They were magnificent. He could understand why someone with a pair of sharp scissors might be tempted to trim a little above the eyes so the animal could see better. But why were domestic animals in the zoo? He didn't dare ask anyone.

He looked around. He and Mac were alone. The zoo would be closing in about thirty minutes and families had headed for a final look at the more traditional big ticket items, like Frankie the Chimp, or the baby giraffe, whose birth had been streamed live on Facebook. The interns had watched.

Mac looked around also, and smiled. "Hand me the bag," he said.

"Here sweet babies," he said, proffering his outstretched palm. "Come to daddy for a trim."

The Highland Cow stepped forward, followed by the sheep with incredibly curly horns. Basil couldn't tell if brown cows could see Mac, or just heard his cooing, or if they smelled his special food.

He felt an unfamiliar exhilaration, as he watched Mac extract a small pair of shears from his jacket pocket.

"Basil," whispered the barber, "I would be honored if you take the first snip."

Basil's stomach lurched. The always-perfect citizen's proper response was quickly losing out to "go-ahead-and-do-it." Mumbling carpe diem, he looked around, even up to see if there was a camera facing the pen, stepped forward, accepted the scissors, and snipped a lock from the cow's bangs and a curl from under the sheep's chin.

He handed the scissors back to Mac and pocketed the lock and curl. A small smile played across his face. Shirley would never believe it. Amanda would be horrified.

"Hey, Mac," said a loud voice behind him. It was one of the zoo's security men. "Aren't you Mac the Barber?"

Mac slid his shears up his sleeve. "People often ask that," Mac replied curtly. "I drive A cab."

"Too bad," said the chatty guard. "I was hoping I'd meet him some day. He has one helluva reputation. Take the way he walked out of his shop leaving some stupid bloke half-lathered in the chair. I howled when I saw it on the news. Mac must have had a good reason, and it makes me want to be like him. To just walk out my job some day too. Maybe I'd be working at the airport and I'd be in the middle of frisking a little old lady who might have a gun. TSA would let her pass without removing her shoes, but I'd make her take them off and maybe more. And while she's standing there in her hose, I'd just walk away. Just like Mac. Fifteen minutes till closing, fellas. Have a good day."

Mac waited until the guard was out of view, then resumed his trimming, occasionally offering more treats to the drooly tongues.

When shiny dark eyes appeared on both groomed faces, Mac tossed the rest of the food into the pen. "That's IT for now. We'll be back."

He handed Basil the cloth bag and the rest of the trimmed wool. "We'd better get out of here." He popped most of the remaining homemade treats in his mouth.

"That was quite a tribute to you," said Basil. "Even though that guy was wrong about why you left."

"What do you KNOW about it?" asked Mac.

"Wasn't it something you were watching on TV?"

"Mind your own business," said Mac, but he sounded amiable rather than annoyed.

Basil decided not to pursue Mac's reasons while he was still carrying sharp objects. He also realized that if the zoo was closing, he was missing yet another briefing with Sangria about the Kenly Pope's increasingly turgid book. Sangria had probably been on the phone with Shirley and Amanda at least once or twice and they may have called the police by to report him missing.

"I guess I should go home now," he said.

Mac checked the meter. "Don't worry about the fee for today. Like I said, I gotta tab running for you. We'll settle up later, buddy. Want me to pick you up tomorrow at lunch? I got some other places to show you."

Basil hesitated. "I really have work to catch up on."

"Okay," said Mac, glancing at him through the mirror. "I'll be at your building at two. We can have a late lunch at Rudy's."

Amanda opened the apartment door after Basil repeatedly knocked. "Mom is very upset with you," she whispered. "Very."

"I'm fine," said Basil, "as you can see, and I'm an adult who doesn't need monitoring."

"Your recent actions belie that," said his daughter, motioning at him to remove his shoes. "Just where have you been? Your clothes smell of wild animals. I hope you weren't buying leather or meat. By the way, Sangria is furious. She had to cuddle Cleopatra all afternoon and now she's ordered a rooster."

Basil cleared his throat and said, "I went to see an allergist." He took a tentative step toward the kitchen then realized that Oscar Wilde preceded him.

"Damn cat!" he shouted He yanked off his socks and tossed them in the laundry basket.

"Is that you, Basil?" asked Shirley. "I've had a drinky-poo without you. Your day has been stressful again for me."

Sounds more like three or four poos, thought Basil. *Shirley sounds slurry.*

He poured a port. A large one.

"Where were you all afternoon? I'm tired of getting calls from your office this week. I'm not your secretary." The drinky-poos had taken over. Amanda sat close to her mother on the couch. They waited for Basil's explanation.

"Everything's fine. Really. And I'll be able to stay better in touch when I have a phone I can figure out, new credit cards and my ID."

Amanda arched an eyebrow. "Not buying it, Dad." He shrugged. They sat in silence. He studied his glass, avoiding their gazes.

"Oh, but he's right," said Shirley finally. *She sighed, a bit dramatically,* Basil thought. "He's gone through a lot this week. Amanda, call Sangria and let her know that he has been found and he will be in, on time, in the morning."

Basil's fingers slipped into his pocket and stroked the snippet of coarse wool and cow's hair. "And you can tell her that I will be out tomorrow afternoon at two."

7

Basil had barely opened the manuscript when he was summoned to Sangria's office. This time he was prepared. On his way to work he had stopped at Grayley's Neighborhood Drugs with a big RX sign blinking above the front door. The store could not compete with the national drugstores a few blocks away, but Grayley's was conveniently on the way to work. Grayley had died about fifteen years ago, and his store had been purchased by the VanderPrats—a very nice family, who owned several buildings and apartments on the block.

Basil bought a purple washcloth to dampen then breathe into, and in case that didn't help, a mask to wear during his meetings with Sangria and her flock. He also purchased, despite the expiration date from a decade earlier, eye drops guaranteed to help those with allergies.

So when Sangria called, Basil dribbled drops from the over-the-counter ocular anti-allergen, and opened the main office door. The interns quieted as he passed through their cubicle area. There was a bounce in his step as he contemplated leaving at two for another ride with Mac. It had been a long time since he had greeted each of his staff members by name, he realized, looking into their curious eyes or blank stares as he passed them. That wasn't good management. He needed to make changes in his last weeks—to show them that he cared despite their work ethics. If only they had felt the hair of the Highland Cow, they would see life differently. Names tomorrow; pleasant nods today.

Sangria was pacing with Cleopatra tucked under her arm when Basil knocked and entered. "What have you got over your face? What's that purple thing?"

"Wasbleclth," he said through the damp terry.

"I can't meet with you looking like that," she said. "You are raising my stress level."

"Neddltobreethe," said Basil.

Cleopatra cocked her head, and clucked.

"You're upsetting her and Orange Julius," said Sangria.

"Ornglusius?"

"Her new consort," said Sangria. His full name is Orange Julius Caesar. His pedigreed show name was Orange Julius, and I added the Caesar because it went with Cleopatra. If you'd take that purple rag off your face you'd be able to see him."

Basil dropped one corner of the cloth so he could peek. A small, extremely feathery orange rooster was perched on the top of Sangria's computer.

"It's a Pekin," said Sangria. "Another rescue bird. Very friendly. Perhaps had been a family pet. What do you think?"

"Vryfhery," said Basil. His nose was itching and his eyes were burning.

"That's what I thought you would say," she said. "Have a seat. We need to talk."

Basil inched his way through the office, past Cleo's pen now enlarged to accommodate Orange Julius.

"Basil, I know your days are numbered. I didn't mean to put it quite that way," said Sangria, "but there is a major book project to complete, as you know, and I have one more task that will take up some of your time. Just an itty-bitty amount, though." She was silent, awaiting a response. There was none.

"Can you hear and understand me through that purple cloth?"

"Yzvrywel."

"Then we are in agreement?"

"Wzthtsk?"

"If you are asking about the nature of the task, I'm embarrassed that I am understanding you in this ridiculous conversation. You will be in charge of setting up the office petting zoo. I've been reading up on this and it's becoming all the rage."

Basil could no longer suppress a sneeze, which was captured by the cloth across his face.

Sangria continued, "I want you to follow up with the staff in all departments about what animals or creatures, such as lizards or snakes, would give them comfort. We'll set up the selections in the basement storeroom, which is being remodeled as we speak. You can also think of a good name for it. Something inclusive but catchy."

Basil nodded. "Ndtgo," he said.

"Have a proposal for me by tomorrow morning, Basil. I'm sure this will be a big hit."

"Wlldu," he said. He was relieved that Sangria hadn't mentioned his progress, or lack of it, with the book.

He washed his face in the men's room on the way back to his office and picked small feathers off his jacket. They seemed magnetically drawn to the fabric.

By the time he returned to the staff area, he felt surprisingly sunny. He nodded to Samantha and told her that he would be leaving at two for an important meeting out of the building. She did not press for details. He looked at his interns, paid and unpaid, who had come to O.O.&O. with such eagerness and enthusiasm months or years earlier. Willym, Sari, Nadia, Jakob, Abi, Morgan, Lester, Den, Marni, Len, Babsun, Aquelle, and the rest. He had called only one meeting with them in the last year to discuss new rules on fact-checking. It was no longer their job. It was totally up to the authors to make sure everything was accurate. "Too time consuming and costly," Sangria had said. Just look for typos that might embarrass the firm.

Basil had thought that edict was a mistake. Authors, if they hadn't known what they wrote was incorrect, wouldn't be able to judge if it were incorrect, such as misspellings of names. Shouldn't editors correct, or at least bring to the attention of an author that Katharine Hepburn's name had an "a" in it rather than misspelled it as "Katherine"?

And with the Internet at their fingertips, couldn't the interns quickly look up dates and names on credible websites? It was a new world and one he would be leaving soon. One last book, and now one more project.

He would call another department meeting, but tomorrow, not this afternoon. Mac would be waiting.

Mac wasn't waiting. Basil watched up and down the street. He paced. He wanted to check his watch but it still wasn't working. He went back into the lobby to check the time on the digital wall clock near the elevator: 2:15. The revolving door opened and Sangria stepped out. "Taking a late lunch?" she asked.

"You might say that," replied Basil, trying to sound offhand and pleasant.

"I will have lots of surprises to show you at five," she said.

"I won't be back," said Basil, wishing she had heard him as the doorman whistled for a Yellow Cab for her.

Mac was still nowhere to be seen. Basil sat on a wooden bench near the fifteen-foot high (not including the granite base) bronze family statue of Old Man Ozburn holding a thick closed book, its title unreadable after years of exposure to the city weather, pigeons, and grime. Next to him, her arm on his and face uplifted in homage, was his wife, Margarita, and sitting on stacks of books at his feet, were the adoring little Ozzies. All the years that Basil had passed this family memorial, he had never really studied it. He knew that vandals, rumored to be disgruntled clerks from many years earlier, had occasionally sprayed it with insulation foam, but he had never paid much attention. Now he had time to really scrutinize this pretentious piece. Hardly a tourist attraction, yet, as he waited for Mac, three tourists speaking Norwegian took his picture with the statue in the background, and a mixed group of tourists with a guide, pulled out selfie sticks.

He saw that past vandals had painted Sangria's lips purple and that someone had scaled the statue to cover OMO's hair with orange paint. Removal efforts had not been totally successful. Newer yellowish-white spots were contributed by the pigeons.

He scanned the street once again for a sign of Mac's cab. He hated to go back to the office and admit he had been stood up. That hadn't happened since his senior prom when he had invited Hillary Rooney, a math whiz who was going to the University of Pennsylvania in the fall. She wasn't home when he came to her house with an orchid corsage—the kind that strapped on a wrist. Her father answered the door, surprised. He seemed even more surprised when Basil mumbled his mission—that Hillary was his prom date.

"She didn't mention it to us," said the man. "She's out."

Basil hesitated. It was far to late to ask anyone else to go with him. The prom would begin in an hour. He had rented a tux. Paid for the tickets. Borrowed his father's car. Filled the tank with gas.

Mr. Rooney waited a moment then said, "Good night. I shall tell her someone called."

Basil was about to hand him the corsage, but the door had closed. He tossed it on the front porch, hoping she would find it and be embarrassed. He never mentioned the flowers or asked where she had been when they sat next to each other in math on the following Monday.

He'd give Mac a few more minutes, then gave up at three. When he returned to his office, Samantha was on the phone. The staff room was quiet. His warthogs were engaged in new bizarre acts, even for warthogs.

8

"I've poured our drinky-poos," Shirley said, "and Amanda will be late for dinner. She had an errand to run. I can't understand all her new interest in animals. I think she's volunteering at rescue mission or something."

"Everybody's suddenly interested in animals," muttered Basil as he removed his tie and prepared to slip into his lounging clothes and slippers.

"What did you say?" called Shirley.

"Nothing. I'll be right in."

"I took Oscar Wilde to get his nails clipped today and to get his wellness exam and planned to set his neutering appointment, and you'll never guess what they told me."

"What?" asked Basil settling down in his recliner with his port.

"Guess!"

"He has ingrown toenails?"

"No. Guess again."

"He has fleas?"

"No, he's pregnant."

"He can't be pregnant!"

"That's the point. He's a she. It's like that with cats sometimes," said Shirley. "When we adopted him, he was small and well, rather furry, and I guess they missed it."

"How could they miss it? Aren't they supposed to know what they are handing out at a pet event?" He thought back to the day about eight months earlier when Amanda had prevailed on her parents to go with her to Petstravaganza at a mall pet shop. The rescue group was inundated with kittens and cats and was determined to find homes for all of them by day's end. A TV crew was there to film the last batch to be adopted. Young volunteers wearing orange T-shirts inscribed with Petstravaganza rushed up to potential adopters and extolled the virtues of each animal.

"We don't need a new animal," Basil reminded them several times, but Amanda asked them simply to consider a replacement for Olivia Newton John, their calico that had disappeared on New Year's Day after five years of hiding in Basil's closet.

Basil had not missed that cat. She was not a seasonal shedder; she was constant. But Shirley said she'd consider just the right kitten, and Amanda, who couldn't keep one in her apartment, was overjoyed. By the time they arrived at the adoption event, most of the cats and kittens had been spoken for. They spotted the little fox-colored animal, one of two kittens left. And while the TV cameras rolled, Amanda and Shirley were interviewed on air about how rescue animals make wonderful pets. The kitten tucked its head under Shirley's jacket and purred. Basil knew that his wife and daughter had made a decision without his input.

"What will you call this cute little boy?" asked Allison Yager, the TV interviewer.

"You name him, Dad," said Amanda. "Something literary. And this will be your kitten."

Basil thought for a moment. Too long a moment.

"How about Oscar Wilde," said Shirley. "My husband's in publishing, you know. He's an editor at Ozburn, Ozburn & Ozburn."

Basil was glad that the TV crew did not jot down anything about his work. He did not want any discussion about this at his office.

"And his twin, the last little ball of fluff, is going home with me," announced Allison. "Our viewers will love to watch the kitten-cam we'll set up in the newsroom."

And so they brought little Oscar home. Shirley reminded Basil that the cat would be his, tuned into the interview on TV that night, and assumed his maleness which, as Basil thought back, had been bestowed upon the kitten by none other than Allison Yager. The cat rescue people had packed up empty cages and were leaving the pet store by the time Oscar had been named. No one had corrected Allison. No one had thought to flip him over to have a close look.

Oscar Wilde was due to be neutered after he was six months old. Shirley made sure he had his kitten shots, but the vet was on vacation when six months rolled around. Shirley promised to schedule it soon. However she was increasingly occupied by yoga, tai chi, beginning pickleball and her garden club activities.

"So, how did Oscar get pregnant?" Basil asked. He reached for the decanter and topped off his glass.

"How do we all?" asked Shirley with a sly laugh.

"I mean, isn't he indoors all the time?"

"I have no idea," she answered. "Things happen when the cleaners are here."

"When is he due?"

"In about two weeks. I thought he was just getting fat, but . . ."

"Why didn't anyone tell us?"

"What difference does it make, dear? Would you have rejected the poor kitten if he had been female?"

"Do we have to change his name?" Basil asked.

Shirley waited to respond. "I'll leave that up to you."

Basil closed his eyes. Why was everything so complicated. Life was simple when he was younger. Before his wives. Before his daughters. Before Oscar Wilde. Before Sangria and the steady supply of staff/internists Sangria hired. He thought of his boyhood home. Small town New England. Kids did chores, got allowances, had painted turtles, and beagles. Mothers stayed home, made triple-chocolate pudding and oatmeal cookies. Had a ready supply of Band-Aids and Mercurochrome. Vicks VapoRub. Comfort everything. That wasn't his mother, of course. That was Alfred's mother. Alfred lived next door and had both dogs and cats and a painted turtle that lived in a plastic dish with a plastic palm tree impaled in a plastic island. Alfred had a cookie jar that was always full, and received a generous allowance for doing not much of anything as far as Basil could tell, and a beagle named Howly.

"Basil, what do you think?" Shirley persisted.

"Keep it," said Basil. "No point in wasting a good name. Have you told Amanda about the kittens?"

"She's elated. She's planning a shower."

"For Oscar?"

"For the kittens. There is so much they will need. Besides kitten kibble and little bell collars, they will probably need some dresses."

"Gawd, I don't believe it," said Basil.

"Don't you remember how she liked to dress her cats? It was so cute."

Unfortunately, Basil did.

"She's already been in touch with Allison Yager. Allison and her crew will be documenting everything as a follow up to the adoption festival."

"Gawd." Basil let the warmth of the liquid rise to his temples. "Perhaps, Ms. Yager can help us find homes for the litter."

"How could you suggest that?" asked Shirley. "Really, Basil, you are talking about Oscar's babies before they are born and you already are giving them away. I'm shocked."

Oscar Wilde waddled into the room, and coughed near Basil's slippers. It was not a good sign. Basil closed his eyes. It would be better to continue the discussion another day. He did not plan to be home whenever the shower was scheduled. He would have Mac take him for a ride somewhere. Anywhere.

Basil barely looked in the mirror before he left for work. He knew he should have stopped with one large before-dinner port, but when Amanda arrived with packages from Lucky Pets, he uncorked a bottle of Merlot and ate his "pork" tofu stir fry in silence. He tied his tie from memory, smoothed back wisps of graying hair, and headed out. Shirley was still in bed. She and Amanda had stayed up late chatting in the kitchen. He had muted their discussions with his second pillow, the one Oscar Wilde considered his own. Basil was having difficulty thinking of Oscar as a female, but there were other literary people whose names did not match their gender, such as George Sands. Perhaps the cat should be renamed Amantine Lucile Aurore Dupin, or Vyvyan, a rather gender-neutral name today, but was the moniker of the real Oscar's second son. Why was Basil even thinking about his cat?

When he arrived at his office, Basil realized that he had brushed past the interns without seeing them and was standing behind the desk. Sticky notes with messages plastered the surface. Most were from Sangria demanding updates, then canceling meetings because of media appointments. He sat. One note caught Basil's attention. Mac had tried to reach him after he had gone home for the day. "Meter's still running," it said. "I waited and you weren't there."

Basil rubbed his temples again, wishing he had taken two aspirin instead of just one with his coffee. He had no idea how to reach Mac and the meter was still running. He would never be able to retire by the time he paid Mac's tab. Maybe he had the day wrong. Yes, that might be it. He'd go back to the bench at two today, and Mac would drive up and honk. Meanwhile, he'd look at another chapter or two of Kenly Pope's manuscript.

The plot hadn't made sense for several chapters. The unlikely romance between Ash and Dresden was at a standstill since Dresden had lost his smart phone, and the police had found it. He didn't have a security lock on it so the police looked at the photographs he had taken of Ash during their first passionate night at the only cheap motel out of town. His interrogation had not gone well, especially when Ash said she had not given him permission for anything. She had joined some movement with a hashtag.

"Trash," muttered Basil.

"What?" asked Darwin.

Basil looked up, surprised. "I didn't hear you knock."

"I didn't knock. I coughed loudly because your door was open. You left it open. I wondered if I should close it and knock, or leave it open and cough," Darwin replied.

Basil studied the young man. He reminded him of himself at that age, whatever age, Darwin was. Tall, serious. A cold sore on his upper lip just under his nose, red and as large as a dime. Blue-gray eyes.

"Yes, have a seat."

Darwin looked around. There was no guest chair. "I'll go get mine," he said, returning quickly with an ergonomic one on wheels.

I had an extra chair last week, thought Basil. *I know I did.*

Darwin wheeled close, but not too close, to Basil's desk.

"Mr. Beale," he said.

"Yes, how can I help you?" Darwin was clearly nervous.

"Mr. Beale, I've been working here for six years and I've never had a raise. I would like a raise, and also, something to do. You haven't given me anything to do in a long time."

Basil was puzzled. It was times like this that he hated being in management. He didn't like supervising people, correcting behaviors, or dealing with personnel issues, such as office politics. He himself was underpaid, but felt that his bosses, the Ozzies, should be able to make those decisions without being asked. They would know what they could afford and what he was worth. It was impolite to ask. This new generation didn't have the same values. And now, nice quiet Darwin was putting him on the spot. If Darwin got a raise, the rest of the interns would want one too. Basil would have to deal with Sangria on his staff's behalf. She would be annoyed at him. On the other hand, his staff might have an uprising or threaten to join a union if he didn't speak up for them. It would be ugly either way. And in his last few weeks.

Darwin watched him for a reaction. Basil tapped his red pen, then pulled out a sheet of paper. He would appear to be taking notes. His head felt oddly detached from his body as if he were looking through a settling fog. A morning fog that appeared just as you were ready to leave home for the day.

"Something to do?" Basil repeated.

"Yes," said Darwin. "I had a proof-reading project when I first got here and when I finished it, you said I had done a good job and you'd get me something else, and I've been waiting, sir."

"For a year?"

"About three, sir. Some of your other staff might be waiting too."

"And why didn't anyone mention this before?"

"Some were concerned that you might actually give them work. And, I, well, I admired you too much to bother you. I figured you had a plan for each of us."

"A plan. Yes, a plan," said Basil, pleased that someone admired him, but unsure about the plan. He seriously doubted that there had been such a long time between projects. Three weeks at the most. It wouldn't look good if it were true and word reached the Ozzies. They wouldn't mind having low-paid interns not getting paid for doing nothing, but Darwin was one of the better-paid staffers.

"Thank you, Darwin, for bringing both issues to my attention. I will work on them."

As Darwin beamed with relief. Through the port or Merlot murkiness from the previous night, Basil had a thought.

"Darwin, I'm editing a very important manuscript at the moment, an unknown author who is likely to make headlines. I'm wondering if you'd be willing to be part of my elite critique team. Read it and give me written feedback. Not necessarily honest feedback. In fact, positive feedback in writing, but you can certainly tell me the truth behind these closed doors."

"Really? Yes, sir. I'm ready to start. You'll be proud of how fast and accurately I work."

Basil tapped the pages together into a neat stack, and handed them to Darwin. The young man read the title. "What kind of title is this? *The Devine Royalty Social Club Queen's Son*. Shouldn't we change it?"

Basil lifted his finger to his lips. "Shhh. I totally agree, but think positive. It's likely to appeal to readers who love that approach. You know, *The Dog Handler's Wife*, or the *The President's Hookers*. That sort of thing. It's all the rage. Best-seller lists because of the title."

"I get it," said Darwin.

Just as he was about to return to his desk, Basil said, "One more thing, would you be able to look online to see if you can find a phone number for Mac's Cabs?"

"Happy to," said Darwin. "And please let me know about the raise, Mr. Beale. It has been such a pleasure working for you. You are such an, uh, uh, inspiration."

"I will, and oh, Darwin, do you need kittens?" Basil said after the office door closed. He knew it was premature to find homes for Oscar Wilde's offspring, but he needed to practice asking.

He fished around his middle drawer on the left for the aspirin bottle. Gone. In fact, many of his emergency supplies were missing. No antacids (chewable), or gummy vitamins (a silly gift from Mrs. Joyce Royce one Valentine's Day). He missed her. She made him laugh. She had insider information on the Ozzies that she secretly shared with him. She had warned him to watch out for Sangria. He had been able to confide in her about his worries about Amanda. It was when they had accidently met at Honest Abe's Tap Room and had more than one drink. Mrs. Joyce Royce's knee had accidentally leaned into his, causing welcome, but uncomfortable feelings in regions that should have known better. All accidental, of course.

Her knee never moved, and she jingled her gold charm bracelet. Her hand brushed his arm. He nearly wept.

And Mrs. Joyce Royce, with that beautiful silver hair piled in an enormous bun, held in by a mother-of-pearl and gold comb, with her low-cut red blouse, and shiny, perfectly tapered fingernails, a matching red. In a movie-star throated voice, that he had never heard her use at work, she said, "Basil, I think we should go home now."

"Your place?" asked Basil.

"No dear, our separate ways tonight," said Mrs. Joyce Royce, kindly. She looked at her watch. "Shirley will be looking for you, and I have to feed my guinea pigs."

Basil wanted to ask their names, anything to keep the thrilling moment alive, but Mrs. Joyce Royce had slipped into her light jacket, red, with pockets. She said good night, blew a kiss, and rushed out the door, leaving him to pay for the drinks.

It hadn't been terribly long after that incident that Basil learned that Mrs. Joyce Royce had received a promotion and was now the office manager at one of The Towers. The big Towers. At her farewell, an elegant affair she said to Basil, "Call me and we can do lunch some day."

By then, he had read that such behavior could be interpreted as inappropriate, even if they were just friends "doing" a platonic lunch. He had never "done lunch" with anyone and wasn't sure what that entailed. He never called. In fact, he didn't know how "to do lunch" especially at his age. It was one thing to go to Rudy's with Mac. Mac? Where was Mac when he needed him.

Basil stood up and looked out through his office door window at Darwin, who was seemingly studying the manuscript. Had he forgotten to search for Mac's Cabs? Maybe it should be Mac's Cab. He might only have one. Or perhaps Mac had a different name for his business. Darwin looked up and saw Basil's face. He held up his pointer finger to signal "just a moment," then scribbled something and brought it to Basil's door. It was a phone number.

"Apparently the company's name is MacCabbie," said Darwin. "I verified it by calling and some guy named Alto answered. He's the dispatcher. I hope you don't mind that I told him you needed a pick up at two. He wouldn't let me off the phone until he arranged a ride for you."

Basil thought for a moment. This was an unexpected turn, but why not.

"Thanks, Darwin."

"Don't forget the raise," said the young man.

"I'm working on it," said Basil. He sat back at his desk and looked at the clock. He felt a burden had been lifted. With his business experience, Mac would be able to tell him how to handle Darwin's salary request. Mac would also know what to do about Oscar Wilde, and the whole business about the comfort animals. So would Mrs. Joyce Royce. He wondered if she still pushed up her thick hair in a poofy bun. Were her long nails that clicked on her keyboard still painted with tiny red hearts or snowmen on Valentine's Day and Christmas?

Yet, he was increasingly annoyed with Mrs. Joyce Royce for creeping into his thoughts when Shirley was the love of his life and they would soon be spending all day together when he retired. Panic set in again. What would he do in just a few weeks? Shirley would be off for the day with her clubs and shopping and lunch with Amanda or her friends. He had no day plans. Shirley would no longer set out his ties and socks to match his suits. She might not even fix breakfast. She would expect him to take care of himself. He would read the morning papers, and maybe stay in his pajamas. Perhaps he would take a walk. He would cleanup after Oscar Wilde and look in the classifieds to see if anyone actually was looking for kittens. He might write a letter to the editor about something or give Mac a call for a ride. He had seen people his age, prematurely retired, cheerfully bagging groceries at the local supermarket, just for something to do. A former school superintendent had told him to join him bagging at the checkout.

Basil rubbed his chin. Perhaps, if he approached her properly, Sangria would let him take back his retirement letter, even though she written it for him. He could find that allergist and get the right medications so that he could offer to take care of Sangria's chickens or whatever else she might house in her office. He was startled by the intercom buzzer, and then Samantha's voice. "Someone to see you, Mr. Beale. He says he's tired of waiting."

What was this about? Basil had no scheduled appointments. He quickly rose and adjusted his gray pin-striped tie as the door to his office opened, and Mac burst inside.

"There you are," said Mac, with both annoyance and awe. "I've been waiting for two days. Nice digs, you have."

Basil sputtered, "But I was waiting for you outside. You were supposed to..."

"Bygones," said Mac. "You got a tab with MacCabbie, so it's okay. Are you ready? But first, I gotta to try your chair. Gotta see what it feels like to be the boss of so many people out there."

He slipped into the chair and swiveled it around. "Not bad, but you really need something new. This one is pretty frazzled, old man, and you look like you really need a haircut."

Basil studied his former barber, hoping he didn't have any tools in his pockets. Mac was wearing a soft black leather jacket with a patch with his company name. Visible at the neckline was a red T-shirt that also looked brand-new, and he was wearing crisp blue jeans and orange sneakers. His hair wisped out from under a shiny chauffeur's cap.

"New clothes?" asked Basil as he reached for his coat.

"Yep. My tabs and tips are very promising, so I'm upgrading my work wardrobe, just like I did at the barbershop. Ready to go?"

"Yes, it's early, but I'll just let the front desk know." Basil remembered all too well about Mac's extra-large barber apron, new in the days before he had vanished. Striped like the red, white, and blue pole outside his shop, with his name in large red swirls on the top. It had large reinforced pockets for his various blades, scissors, and combs. Had he known that because of the extra-large size the length would come to his knees. He might have had it further customized, he told his customers. Most clients privately agreed, but told him how great it looked. He had the blades and straps, after all. When Mac left Basil in the chair that day, cursing and running out the door, Mac was still wearing his apron tied neatly around his corpulent waist—an impressive imitation of an armed, lunatic human barber pole heading down the street. It was still astonishing that he hadn't been arrested or at least institutionalized for a brief period. Or perhaps he had. Basil had never heard.

Basil took the elevator to the lobby. Mac was double-parked by the entrance to O.O.&O. Basil started to open the door to the back seat.

"Hey, Baz, sit up front with me," called Mac. "Won't cost extra this trip. You'll be like the copilot."

Mac pulled his logbook closer to his lap, and tossed newspapers and empty paper cups into the back.

"Where to, buddy?" asked Mac, hitting his horn as he pulled out into traffic without looking.

Basil still foggy from the prior night's poor judgement with Shirley's drinky-poos, said, "Where to is fine with me."

Mac said, "Well then, hang on." He stepped on the gas, sped through a light as it changed to red.

Basil fished for his seat belt. There wasn't one. "Meant to get that fixed," said Mac, "but there's quite a cost. Too many regulations anyway. I'm counting on a lot of them GOING away." He gave Basil a look. "Don't you agree, Baz? Too many rules. #TooManyRules. I'm part of a new movement. Don't follow rules you don't agree with. Makes sense." Basil stifled a gasp as Mac made a left turn from the right-hand lane onto a one-way street. He clutched the side of the seat.

"But aren't some important?"

"Nah. Not REALLY. I learned to drive from my uncle Sal, a cabbie in Boston. He showed me how to merge with your eyes closed when you went from six lanes to one going through a tunnel. Stuff like that.

Everyone got out of his way. Works like a lucky charm. That's why I have this rabbit foot." Mac pointed to a dangly furry object hanging from his rearview mirror. It was part of a collection of small hanging objects that could easily block the driver's view: a pair of dice, a four-leaf clover air freshener which may have been used to swat flies, a picture of the pope (not this one), and a dog-eared photo of a nude woman. Basil didn't remember noticing it before. For a moment he thought the woman resembled Mrs. Joyce Royce. That couldn't be possible. He looked away, wishing he had insisted on being the backseat passenger rather than Mac's copilot.

"I knew you'd agree," said Mac. "There are too many regulations. Wear and tear on tires. Ethanol. Brake inspections. It should be up to each cabbie to decide what makes a CAB safe. No nip behind the wheel? What's wrong with texting? See what I mean? Why did God make SMART phones if you can't use them when you want?" He pointed to the check-engine light that was flashing red.

"Who invented that annoying light? Next thing you know they'll make the car stop and fix itself. To hell with that. And that's just the start. I was going to take you again to Rudy's today for his peanut butter special but, too many regulations. The health department shut him down. That's nuts and wrong. They have no business going into his kitchen with white gloves and then complain that the gloves get greasy when they rub their prying fingers on his cooktop. Land of the not free!"

Basil closed his eyes. He wanted to put his fingers in his ears.

"Stupid regulations everywhere. How many items you can take to the grocery store's express register. How much money you can charge to your credit card. How many calories in a candy bar. What's next? How many times you can go to a BARBER in a year? The world has gone mad. Did you have lunch yet?"

"No, that would be nice."

"I got an idea. Let's go to My Little Chicken. My cousin Coleen and her partner run it. Don't ask about them. Don't get me going."

"I won't," promised Basil. He was suddenly afraid of the possibility of feathers.

"And no matter what pretend you don't notice her chin hairs. I used to trim them but she's been turning me down lately. Says I charge too much."

Coleen was behind the lunch counter, a smart phone tucked under her bristled chin. She turned to flip a grilled cheese sandwich on the stovetop behind her. There was a physical resemblance to Mac. She was short, a bit bulky, and wearing a red, white, and blue striped apron that had seen better days. It was familiar. Somebody had stitched fabric over the words barbershop, but left "Mac," then penned "and Cheese" after it.

"Yeah, yeah, yeah," said Coleen, then hung up. "Crap. Crap. Crap."

"Whuz up?" asked Mac, leaning on the counter.

"Have a seat anywhere," she said, giving Basil the once over.

"What'll it be, bud?" Her dark eyes flashed. Her thick hair reminded him of Mrs. Joyce Royce.

"I haven't seen a menu yet," said Basil, with his most pleasant smile, so as not to offend.

"Oh, right. Grilled cheese is our special today," said Cousin Coleen.

"Make it two," said Mac, "and put it on his tab."

He nodded to Basil to follow him to the last seats at the counter. Unlike Uncle Rudy's, the counter seemed to have been washed in the last week, and there was real tableware. That was a promising start. Coleen slid a spatula under a sandwich, which had blackened and was smoking. She tossed a limp dill pickle on the plate and carried it to a man reading a newspaper in the back of the room. The customer was clearly not pleased and their voices rose.

"So, whaddah ya want me to do? Feed it to the pigeons? Scrape it off and stop complaining. Geez." Coleen muttered, "Crap," as she stomped back to the counter.

Mac leaned close to Basil. "Don't say anything about the food. She's very sensitive about her cooking."

Basil decided to order the grilled cheese on the rare side. But he knew it probably wouldn't matter to Coleen.

"So, Cuz, I thought I'd see you at Leo's last Sunday. GOOD party."

"Don't ask," replied Coleen. "Here." She placed their meals in front of them on the counter. The bread was burned, just as Basil suspected.

He said nothing, but wondered if he could scrape it off without causing problems.

Coleen did not move back toward the cooktop. She leaned on her elbows and studied Basil's face while he surveyed his sandwich.

"I know you from somewhere. TV. Yes, I saw you on TV. You are that funny guy with the chicken."

"Not my chicken," said Basil.

"Yeah, but you were part of that TV stunt. Your boss made you walk into her chicken coop office. Good sport you were."

Good sport? Not.

"Missed it," said Mac. He tapped his sandwich against his plate to knock off the char.

"You can eat here anytime," said Coleen. "A TV personality in my place. Wait till I tell Ricco."

"How's RICCO?" asked Max.

"Don't ask," said Coleen.

When she turned back to her cooking, Basil pried open his blackened sandwich, and scooped out what melted cheese he could with a spoon. He quickly repositioned the toast and looked around the restaurant for a trash basket. Seeing none, he slipped the uneaten blackened bread into his pocket and excused himself. Rather than having Coleen find the remains in the men's room trash basket, he broke into little pieces and flushed. And flushed. And flushed. The water began to rise in the bowl. Basil frantically looked for a plunger. There was none. He knocked on the women's room door. "Not done yet," called a voice from within.

The water crested at the top of the bowl, with no signs of draining. What could he use in place of a plunger to break the clog. It couldn't be due to just his sandwich. Countless other customers had probably tried to flush the evidence of a bad meal. His shoe. Maybe his shoe should work. He slipped out of his right shoe, took a deep breath, and shoved the shoe in the toilet, up and down up and up and down. Soggy crumbs sloshed over the edge of the bowl. He heard Mac called to him through the locked door. "Hey, Baz, are you okay? We're getting worried about you, bro."

"Don't ask," said Basil. "I'll be out soon. Have pie on my tab."

He pumped his shoe again and again. Finally there was a welcome sucking sound as the clog dislodged. He wiped the floor as best he could with toilet paper, and rinsed his shoe in the sink. He wished there were paper towels in the dispenser to blot dry his footwear.

The only telltale sign as he returned to his seat was a watery trail on the linoleum. Mac was chatting with Coleen. She looked as if she might smile, but then scowled. "Don't ask. How may times do I have to tell you!"

"C'mon, Baz. We've got places to go."

Basil gave a feeble wave to Coleen, hoping she wouldn't invite him to return. He much preferred Rudy's.

"Coleen's got the best cheese," said Mac. "Your sandwich disappeared fast. For a minute I thought you threw it out, but you are an honorable man, and practically a member of my family," said Mac, pulling out into traffic and narrowly missing a garbage truck. "And if you hadn't noticed, everything about my family is politically incorrect. All stereotypical. Right out of a seventies sitcom. That's why they got loyal customers. Take Cousin Coleen. She fits the picture of a dumb-broad waitress, but she has a Ph.D. in micronanos from UVA. And Rudy, he got a chef's diploma from Johns and Whales, or whatever they call that cooking school. And me? Top of my class at Waterbury Barbery. Nothing but the best for our family. You can't do any better than our family."

He did a U-turn causing two cars to ride the sidewalk. Basil crouched behind the seat.

"Now, what dija WANT to talk about?" asked Mac.

For a moment Basil's mind was blank. Then it came back to him. "Several things," said Basil. "Could we find a place, like a park, where we could just sit?" Mac ran another red light and honked at pedestrians who had the right of way. They were texting but fortunately looked up at the last second.

"Rules. There should be rules about texting while walking."

"I thought you were against rules," said Basil.

"I have my own," grumbled Mac. He took a shortcut the wrong way down a one-way street. When he saw a delivery truck headed toward them, Basil assumed the crash position and remained there until the cab screeched to a stop at Private Bubba Beauregard Park. The Confederate statue loomed near a fountain that vandals had spiked with dish soap. Then, they had spray-painted a change to the soldier's name, and it became Bubble Beeregaard. This happened at least twice a year and no one, for generations, had been caught.

He spotted an empty wooden picnic table. "There," Basil said. They sat, facing each other.

"So, what's up?" asked Mac. "Work? Home? Hutchy-cutchy?"

Basil said, "Work mostly."

And then as the breeze shifted, and large bubbles blew in their direction, he tested the counseling waters by telling Mac about his conversation with Darwin, and his own looming retirement. And he mentioned the stress animals and his allergies to feathers. He sighed and told him about Oscar Wilde. He did not mention his secret feelings for Mrs. Joyce Royce.

Mac listened carefully, took off his shiny chauffeur's cap and placed it on the table.

"You're asking the wrong person, but it's probably cheaper, EVEN with the meter running, than to sit in a shrink's office. Shrinks can be good. Helped Cousin Alto a lot. But I'll give you my common sense. It's better than my two cents. Ha ha."

Cousin Alto?

"I'd appreciate it," said Basil. He remembered how Mac had offered what had seemed to be solid advice to his customers in the barbershop.

"Well," said Mac. "I wouldn't talk to that boss woman, Sangria, about Darwin's request. She's a featherbrain. Ha ha. Go to one of her brothers. Mano to mano. Ask on behalf of Darwin and also for yourself. What have you got to lose? You're leaving anyway. And don't worry about what to do after retirement. You can always drive a cab. I'm going to grow my company. You can be an investor and an employee. What places we'll go! And about those animals, just turn them loose. Open their cages. Let them be free. That'll cause some stress for boss-lady. But do it on the day you leave. Whata yo got to lose?"

It was all very daring. Some of it made sense, other parts were risky. But, yes, he would take Darwin's request for a raise to one of the other Ozzies.

"Now about the hutchy-cutchy," pushed Mac.

"Never. There has never been any" said Basil, a little too quickly as his face flushed with the thought of Mrs. Joyce Royce. Joyce who may never have been married. His sweet "Bunny," who always told him how nice he looked and showed him pictures of her nine guinea pigs, all named Cuy, often dressed in seasonal outfits.

"I guess we should be going," said Basil.

"Okay," said Mac, with a sigh. "Just remember my offer. You'd look great behind the wheel."

Alto opened the cab's door when Mac double-parked by Basil's building.

"Tomorrow?" asked Mac.

"Call me," said Basil. He turned to the doorman. Alto's face indicated something wasn't right.

"The missus is looking for you. She's worried. You'd better have a good story, about your whereabouts," Alto said.

Oscar, heavy with kittens, tried to escape when Basil opened the door. "Get back. Get back," he shouted, trying to block the cat's exit and maintain his balance.

"Don't shout at Oscar. You'll upset her," called Shirley.

"Sorry," said Basil. "I'll give him extra treats."

"Only the ones labeled "Mother to Be," cautioned Shirley. "We need to talk."

"About Oscar Wilde?"

"No, your daughter."

"Something wrong with Amanda?"

"No. It's Mora."

"Mora?"

"Don't you remember you have a daughter Mora?"

Basil threw his tie and jacket on his bed and kicked off his shoes. He found Shirley in the kitchen. "Of course I do. What about her?"

"She's here."

"Mora here?" The last he had heard, Mora was halfway somewhere around the world. She communicated so infrequently—in fact years had gone by—that, well, he didn't think about her much. His first wife, Margo, had poisoned Mora against him. He tried to reach out when he heard the news about her mother and the avalanche, but there was never any response. "Mora's here?"

"We wanted it to be a surprise. Amanda found her. And it tuns out she was searching for us. Isn't that amazing?"

"Well it sure is," said Basil, rubbing his chin. "I haven't seen her since she was about five, just before Margo defied our custody agreement and whisked her overseas, and they lived under assumed names in Goa or Sri Lanka. Where is she?"

"Amanda is taking her shopping and to a spa. Amanda finds her fascinating—the half-sister she never me until two o'clock today, and you were nowhere to be found when the doorbell rang."

"I was out of the office."

"Well, I know that," said Shirley with annoyance. "Basil, if I didn't know you so well, I'd think you were having an affair. Tell me you're not having an affair." Her eyes puddled.

"Never, my dear," said Basil. "Never." He awkwardly pulled her into his chest.

"Then, where have you been going every afternoon lately? No one in the office seems to know. And that nice young man, Darwin, said you handed off some large project to him—something you've never done before." Her voice bordered on sobs.

"Don't worry, my darling," said Basil, realizing it had been years since he had addressed her this way. "I've been out for fresh air with an old friend—male—Mac the Barber who drives a cab. He's related to Alto, I think."

Shirley's eyes widened with fright. "Not that Mac! Oh no! Alto told me he's dangerous."

"Alto said that? Why would he say that?" Basil asked in alarm.

"You yourself told me that Mac had stormed out of his shop years ago, with all his sharp tools, leaving you lathered and half-shaved in a chair."

"He has his moments but, he's a very insightful person," replied Basil.

"What do you mean he has his moments? So he's only dangerous some of the time?"

Basil couldn't think of anything reassuring. Certainly not Mac's driving. Certainly not trimming hairy animals at the zoo. The job offer to work for his company. And Shirley would have a fit if she knew that his entire retirement income was ticking away in Mac's meter. He felt a queasy panic gripping his gut, then crawling upward until it squeezed his throat.

"I'll try to be careful, my love," murmured Basil into Shirley's hair, suddenly wishing for intimacy he wasn't sure he could muster.

She pushed away. "Is that all you can say? That you'll try? That's not good enough. You could be picked up by the police as an accomplice and spend the rest of your life in the hoosegow."

Basil hadn't' heard that term in a long time, but it was chilling.

"What if I brought him to dinner? You might find him charming," Basil said.

"He's not a new best friend from kindergarten, Basil, or a kitten that followed you home. I don't usually tell you what to do, but you must break off this relationship."

"Break off what?" It was Amanda. They hadn't heard the front door open. Without waiting for an answer, Amanda threw her arms around Basil and said, "Daddy, why haven't you told me more about Mora? We've been having the best time."

Basil turned and there was his older daughter, looking very much like Margo during the good days. Mora reached out her hand as she studied his face. "Hi, Dad." Her voice had a slight accent. Was it Spanish? Or Moroccan? He was uncertain. Her hair was short, boyish, and she had her mother's wide brown eyes and thin lips, and long fingers that were perfect for playing the piano.

"Mora, I've missed you. I wrote and never heard back. I sent gifts Didn't you get any?"

"Mother wouldn't let me contact you. The Sherpas raised me when she passed, but there weren't many reliable mail services in Nepal. Once in a while, I'd get a packet from you, but I had no paper or pen and we needed the paper for our fires to stay warm."

"You poor dear," gasped Shirley. "We had no idea."

"Well, here I am, and if you don't mind, I'd like to stay to get to know all of you. Amanda said it would be okay."

"Of course," said Basil.

"You must be exhausted," said Shirley. "I'll get the guest room ready."

"Oh, she's staying with me," said Amanda. "And the best part, is that after Mora said she'd love to come see us, I talked with Sangria and she immediately offered her a job. It only took a few days for Mora to arrange a flight and here she is."

"Sangria did what?" said Basil, stunned.

"With all Mora's experience working with the Himalayan yaks and goats, she will be an excellent partner in Sangria's Comfort Animals program," bubbled Amanda. "We're just going to give her a day or so to rest up."

"No rest needed," interrupted Mora. "I'm ready to start tomorrow."

"Great, we'll do lunch," said Amanda. "Dad, can she go to work with you? I'll bring her here in the morning and then you can take her around to meet everyone."

"Ah, sure," said Basil. "Great." He wasn't sure he was sure.

The following morning Basil discovered Mora sitting cross-legged on the floor in front of his recliner. Her eyes was closed, her arms folded across her chest, and she swayed as if in rhythm with unheard music. Occasionally her mouth moved and low sounds slipped out and vanished before becoming recognizable. Basil was about to ask if she were okay, but Shirley appeared from the kitchen door and put her finger to her lips, so he tiptoed past.

"What's going on?" he whispered, "and what's this?" Breakfast rarely surprised him anymore, not since Shirley had begun copying Amanda's veganism.

"Fufu," said Shirley.

"No, I mean this," said Basil, pointing to a brownish gob in the bowl in front of him."

"Shh, it's fufu."

His eyes widened in alarm.

"Don't worry. Mora brought a box of it for us to try. It's all the rage."

"Where?" he poked at it with a spoon.

"Well, Africa and the Caribbean," she said. She used her fingers to extract a dab and dipped it in a reddish sauce. "Use your fingers."

"I don't intend to," said Basil under his breath, wishing he had the courage to say those words out loud. "I refuse." It looked like something in Oscar Wilde's cat box.

"It's really quite good," said Shirley. "You won't have the munchies midmorning."

Basil had never wanted a dog more than at this moment. A dog like Alfred's beagle, Howly. Howly always sat under the table and happily inhaled anything that fell or was handed his way. The fufu would have disappeared immediately. Howly never had hairballs either. Or kittens.

"I've really got to hurry," said Basil, looking at the wall clock. "I have to take Mora with me, if she's ready. Bag it up, would you? Will be something to look forward to at lunch time." He was astonished about his brazen subterfuge.

"I'm ready, Dad," Mora said. "What do you think?"

Basil beamed. Mora had the proper professional look for a publishing house employee. For the chief editor's daughter. A long charcoal skirt, yellow silky blouse, casual gray sweater, dangly chain of beads, and matching earrings. No high heels.

"Lovely," said Shirley. "But the furry bag?"

"That was a farewell gift from my Sherpa family. Made from yak balls. I'll never part with it."

"Ready," said Basil. As he headed toward the front door he was forced to do an evasive dance step. "Shirley, Oscar did it again."

Mora followed him down the stairs to the street, where Alto held the door.

"My daughter, Mora," Basil said.

"I know. Met her yesterday before you did," said the doorman.

Basil nodded silently. He and Mora had walked only a few steps when they heard a honk, and a screech of tires. Mac jumped out and opened the cab's door. "At your service," he said, with a wink. Basil wasn't sure if it was intended for him or for Alto.

"We were going to take the bus," Basil said.

"Nonsense, climb in, dear lady."

Mora gave Basil a questioning look, then slipped into the back seat.

"Hotchy-totchy so early in the day? Where to? The Lights Off Motel?"

Basil's face reddened and he said, "To the office. This is my daughter."

"Yeah, I've heard that one before from other customers."

"I mean it!"

"Don't get huffy. I'll drop you off a block from your building so you can pretend all you want."

"I'm not kidding. She's my oldest daughter and she just arrived, and the rest is none of your business."

"Suit yourself. I'll pick you up at two and you can tell me the whole story." He stepped on the pedal and lurched out into the bumper-to-bumper traffic. Mora gasped. She closed her eyes and those little sounds slipped out again.

Basil was relieved when his building came in sight. Mora quickly left the taxi without waiting for Mac to open the door for her. Basil caught up with her when she stopped near the statue of Old Man Ozburn. She pulled her childhood Brownie camera from her yak bag and stepped backward until she could get the perfect vertical shot with her back to the sun.

"I haven't seen one of those in years," said Basil.

"Don't you remember, Dad, you gave this to me for my fifth birthday. It was just before we left. It only took black and white film, but I can't get the film for it anymore, especially in the mountains. So I just take pretend pictures. This is a good one."

"I'll get you a new camera," said Basil. "Whatever you want." He felt very parental with this stranger.

"What will Amanda say?"

"She won't mind at all."

Mora hesitated at the revolving door.

"Don't you remember these?" asked her father.

"Yes, but I didn't have a positive experience," she answered. "Mother yanked me in and my little bunny fur muff became caught and tore to pieces."

"I remember the muff," said Basil. "It was pink. I gave it to you for Christmas just after your birthday."

"White," said Mora. "And I spent my own money on it. I was doing chores at four."

Was that possible? Basil dimly remembered a chart that his wife had posted on the refrigerator every week with chores for little Mora and himself. Dishes, laundry, toilets, cat box. He and Shirley had discussed it briefly when they were dating and had emphatically decided there would be none of that if and when they had a child, although chores did result in children learning responsibility. He certainly did growing up, but not so much Amanda. She hadn't cared if her bed was unmade until fairly recently. Now she was annoyingly neat.

Mora pushed through the revolving door, clutching her furry bag under her arm lest it catch in the moving glass.

She studied the escalator.

"We could take the stairs but the elevator is faster," said Basil heading toward the bank of elevator doors. Mora trailed behind him. He was tempted to ask if she wanted to push the buttons, something she always enjoyed doing as a child, but that might sound inappropriate.

She followed him quietly to his office. Samantha was still on leave, and the newest temp was on the phone, only glancing up when he came in. The interns glanced curiously at Mora and pretended to be working. Basil felt he ought to introduce her, but what to say. He cleared his throat and waited for them to look in his direction.

"Good morning, sir," said Darwin. That alerted the rest of them.

"Good morning," said Basil, gathering his thoughts. "Uh, this is my daughter, Mora, who will be joining the staff at O.O.&O. As of today, she'll be working upstairs with Sangria on special projects."

There were several "welcome Moras," but Darwin, with a worried look, asked, "What sort of special projects? Will that affect any of us or ours?" Realizing that might not have been an appropriate response, he said, "Sorry, that was rude."

"That's okay," said Mora. "I'll be working in the Comfort Animals Division, not in editorial."

The interns clearly showed surprise. "Comfort animals in the plural?" asked Aquelle. "I thought it was just chickens. And that Darwin was doing it."

"Sangria is expanding her options," said Mora, with unexpected authority. "And he has other things to do."

Basil pulled all the new sticky notes, mostly from Sangria's new secretary, Boris, off his door and opened it. Not surprisingly books, chairs, and photos were upside down. The warthogs had been arranged in a circle, as if holding a meeting, and the larger ones seemed to be aiming pencil spears at their leader. *Lord of the Flies* came to mind, while Basil quickly rearranged them to their former docile grouping.

"What are these?" Mora's voice startled him.

"Warthogs. People think I collect them. They give me more and more as presents even though they annoy me."

She slowly surveyed his office. "Why don't you have a picture of me on your desk?" she asked.

"Your mother grabbed them all when she left. Never sent another."

Basil heard that funny little sound again. It was between a whistle, hum and flute.

"I remember the day we packed and left. It was right after she said something bad about your music. She said you were having an affair."

"Not true. Not true at all," said Basil, a bit too defensively. "Shirley was just a friend. She liked my sonatas."

"Mother said she liked them too much. We went to the airport and flew to somewhere—a big city where we changed our names couple of times, then went to the Sherpas."

Basil sighed and busied himself righting his style manuals. It didn't seem to be the right time to tell her his side of the story.

Mora picked up his calendar, the one with vegan recipes that Amanda had placed on his desk.

"You don't have much scheduled today except with someone with the initial M at two. What's this all that about?" asked Mora. "Does M have a name? Did you plan to be with me, Mora? Did Amanda write it on your calendar?"

Basil wished this stranger with the yak purse was less nosy. She increasingly reminded him of the treacherous Margo. But then, what did he expect? Margo had raised their only child with only her version of their relationship. Basil would have to make up for everything now that Mora was in his life. He would locate his sonatas and play for her. He would explain why the marriage hadn't worked. He would buy her another bunny muff, although muff-makers would probably have to use faux fur these days. Maybe real bunny muffs could be located in a vintage shop. Mac might know.

Basil heard the intercom buzz. It was Boris saying that Sangria was expecting Mora to be in her office soon.

"I doubt I'll have time to see you today," said Mora. "Amanda said she's taking me to lunch, and then we'll meet her friends for dinner."

Basil was relieved. "Have a good one. Just take the elevator to the 14th floor."

"I know. Amanda told me." Mora left without saying, "Bye, Dad." That, too, was an odd relief.

Darwin pushed into Basil's office as soon as Mora left. "She's beautiful. You must be very proud of her," he said. "Sorry. I probably shouldn't have commented on her looks, sir. I don't know if that is against company policy."

"We haven't seen each other in a long time," said Basil. "She's changed a lot since I last saw her, which was many years ago when she was very small." He immediately regretted bringing personal information into the conversation. Darwin saw the distant look in his boss's eyes. He cleared his throat "Mr. Beale, I wanted to go over my work on Kenly Pope's manuscript," said Darwin. "You seemed to want a daily update."

"Yes, please," said Basil.

"I'm impressed. Yes, it needs work, but I've been able to edit on screen, and I think you'll like it. I know Kenly will have the final word."

"Actually, maybe not. Sangria makes all relatively unknown authors sign a contract that gives her rights for that, including title and cover."

"I hope she doesn't change the title. It's perfect," said Darwin.

Basil grimaced. But Darwin was fitting in with the Ozzies' plan for this work of crap. Basil decided to ask him to represent him at the morning meeting. Of course, Darwin was bashfully delighted. He reminded Basil about his raise request before returning to his desk. Basil knew he should make an appointment with Howard or Willard about it, but not today.

Basil stayed at his desk during the lunch hour. He planned to leave well before two to meet Mac outside, rather than risk having him come up to the editorial offices again.

The overcast sky foretold possible chilly rain. Shirley had reminded him to carry an umbrella, her Plan B for the weather, but he had forgotten at the last moment when leaving with Mora.

He perched on the edge of the bench under the Ozburns' massive tribute statue. Their sculpted glances were inscrutable. A group Mona Lisa smile. What secrets were behind those faces? Was OMO smiling because he loved his family, or because he had a honey. Or worse.

Basil was immediately embarrassed at the thought. It must have been Mora's words that planted that notion. No, he had insisted that there had been nothing serious going on between him and Shirley prior to his divorce, or rather Margo's abrupt departure. That didn't really explain the birth of Amanda a month before their marriage. Yes, Shirley appreciated his sonatas, and even helped name them when they got together at her loft in an area soon destroyed to make room for the first of The Towers. She was carefree and cheerful and clearly adored him. Brought a bounce to his step and lifted him from his temporary gloom when Margo vanished. She was considerate of his feelings about Mora, saying that she just knew that one day the little girl would seek him out, and even after long years apart, they would have a genuine relationship.

"I will do all I can to be a good stepmother, my darling," said Shirley, squeezing his cheeks.

Warthogs and Feathers

He realized as the years went on that he had ignored Shirley's lack of depth. Her interest in his job had more to do with the occasional office party and the prestige of his title. But her adoration and the nightly port was enough, until Sangria began making his life miserable. Shirley didn't understand his misery. She thought Sangria charming.

Based on his office clock, which he had studied before leaving for his late "lunch," Mac was late again. Basil wasn't sure just how late. He saw a man on the corner spread out a large colorful blanket and arrange objects on it for sale. Basil wondered if working watches were among them. While keeping an eye out for Mac's cab, he wandered over to the vendor. In a neat row behind cell phone covers and turquoise and silver jewelry and colorful seeds and beads necklaces, were watches. The vendor, a squat man in his sixties, was wearing a gray felt pork pie hat, dark glasses, and a frayed plaid jacket.

"How much?" asked Basil, pointing.

"Depends which kind. I have a deal. Genuine Rolex for $15."

"Genuine?"

"Yes. Either digital or regular. You know, the wind-up kind." The salesman, held out samples for Basil's review. Basil was suspicious.

"These can't be Rolex."

"Sure they are. Look at the name." Basil did. The fuzzy printing looked more like Relax, but he couldn't be sure.

"Okay, for you, $10," said the man. "You'll like the wind-up kind. Leather band. Looks more like your style."

Basil fished around in his pocket for his new wallet and extracted a ten. "Tax?"

"Nah. I don't believe in it. Too many regulations. People should only pay what they want. Take this location. I'm not supposed to be here, but who makes all the rules? What difference does it make if I sell my merch where the people are? We all got to work. Take me. I was a bank president until the recession. The market collapsed and the bank closed. So what was I to do? I do better with baubles than bundles of bills." He chuckled, waiting for Basil to laugh with him, but Basil was studying his new watch. He wasn't sure he had made the right decision to buy it. Scammers were everywhere. But this vendor seemed genuine.

"We the people. That's what it's all about. Now, I'm a pretty good judge of character. Knowing you just bought one of my special-deal watches, I can tell you've had hard times too."

Basil didn't respond. He wound the watch and fastened the strap, which looked suspiciously like plastic, around his wrist. But the second hand was moving, and it was clear that Mac was very late.

"Thanks. I'm waiting for someone," Basil said, and turned to go back to the bench in front of his office building.

He passed a police car, and sat at the statue's base again. If only he had brought a book to read. But within five minutes, he heard screeching brakes and honking.

"Get in!" yelled Mac, leaning out the window. He unlocked the front door seat for Basil.

Basil quickly obliged. It was only after the car lurched forward, careening into traffic that Basil sensed there was another passenger. Someone in the backseat.

"Meet my cousin Wiley," said Mac.

Basil turned. The man in the gray felt pork pie hat sprawled over the back seat with his large satchel of trinkets.

"I got a great deal on a straw pork pie for you," said Wiley. "Just what you need for riding around with Mac. And special price. $19.99. Made in China by Rolex."

When Basil hesitated, Mac growled, "Take the deal. He got busted by the cops again. He needs the money for this get-away-in a cab and the $19.99 includes the tip."

Basil handed Mac a twenty, signaled that he didn't want the penny change, and Wiley reached from behind and placed a small straw hat on his head, a hat much like Basil's father's friends wore. He held up a cheap mirror to show Basil.

"Looks good," said Mac, without looking. "You can tip it to the side, to impress your new hottie or pull it down over your forehead a bit for that determined look when you go back to the office whenever. it's time for a meeting with chickens."

The cab lurched into traffic and sped off. Basil heard a siren, then another. He looked back. Cars had pulled off the sides of the congested city street to let the emergency vehicles, and the police, stream through. Wiley appeared to be searching through his satchel of trinkets on the floor. Basil watched the police cars pass the speeding taxi, then slow to force Mac off the road into a side street. Basil pulled his straw hat over his face. Mac cursed in several languages and slammed on the brakes. Basil peeked out from under the brim of his hat and watched a female cop tap on Mac's window, which he reluctantly rolled down.

"Medallion and license," she said.

"Left them HOME, Mele," said Mac.

"Officer to you," said the cop. "It's a ticket this time. Who are your passengers?"

Mac was silent.

Basil thought he better introduce himself.

"Oh, you're from O.O.&O. I heard they're publishing the Kenly Pope novel. Any chance of getting an autographed copy?"

"Sure, I can try," said Basil, "if it's out before I retire."

"Hey," she said, removing her mirror sunglasses, "you're the guy I saw on TV the other night. The guy with the chicken."

"Not my chicken," said Basil.

The officer scribbled some notes, then peered in the back window. "Who's back there?" she asked Mac.

"Cousin Wiley."

"Really? Really? We've been looking for him for over an hour. Selling fake stuff again. Outta the car, Wiley. Mother won't be happy that she's got to bail you out again. Here's your citation." She handed the ticket to Mac.

"Mother?" asked Basil after Wiley and his bag were in the back seat of the patrol car."

"Yeah," said Mac. "Wiley's her brother. She's my cousin. You'd better get her a copy of that book."

Basil felt his new watch slip off his arm. The band was still buckled, but it was no longer attached to the watch. He hoped his hat had a better life expectancy than the timepiece. His stomach was growling. He wasn't sure if it was from hunger, or a gnawing feeling that he shouldn't continue to ride around with Mac. There were moments that he feared things might not end well for either of them. Then again, what was there to worry about? He was in the company of Mac, his former barber, who now had a legitimate job with a license, although Basil hadn't seen it, who got him away from a dreadful office with warthogs, feathers, and Sangria.

If his new watch was correct, at this very moment Sangria was holding another press conference. He had heard from Darwin that during it Sangria planned to show off the new department logo featuring comfort chickens. She said that O.O.&O. would be making brand changes as well, connecting reading to comfort.

There would even be a new self-publishing brand that would appear to look like the books had been published by a Big House. She was considering a comfort porcupine as its emblem. At the suggestion of Kenly Pope, who seemed increasingly to have Sangria's ear, the romance division would be called Chick Lite, with a little peep reading a book while sitting in a heart-shape chair as its new logo. At Darwin provided this information, Basil shook his head. How could the company go so far afield.

He was hungry. He had no idea where they were or what Mac had in mind but he hoped it involved food.

"Let's rob a bank," said Mac, swerving in front of a propane truck that had stopped for a light.

"Oh, no!" shouted Basil.

"Just wanted to see IF you wuz awake," said Mac, "but it might be kind of fun to try. I've been watching old Westerns, and gangster movies. Sometimes there's lots of planning involved and sometimes they just ride up to a bank and say to each other, 'Let's do it now.' And then they'd get one guy to hold the horses, they'd pull their scarfs over their faces and grab their guns and go in and tie up the tellers make everyone fall on the floor, grab sacks of MOOLAH and run out, firing off shots to scare everyone." He grinned at Basil. "Simple, like the good ole days."

Basil said, "It's really not a good idea with all the surveillance today."

"That's why we'd wear disguises."

"Really, not good idea," said Basil. "I don't want to spend my retirement in prison."

"But think about this," said Mac. "If we were successful, you would be in the Virgin Islands or Switzerland with all that money and beautiful girls."

"I'm a happily married man," said Basil. "Remember. I love Shirley."

"Yeah, but you and that honey that rode with me this morning could go off and . . ."

"That's my oldest daughter."

"Oh sure, that's what you said." He didn't sound convinced. "Just think about it. I have lots of ideas. Want lunch?"

"Yes," said Basil, relieved that the subject had changed.

"I'll put it on YOUR tab. Your turn to buy," said Mac.

9

What's on your tie?" Shirley asked when Basil placed his briefcase on the hall table and slipped out of his well-polished shoes.

He looked down, not aware that anything had spilled during his lunch at Buster's Gourmet Souse Café. Mac's cousin, Buster owned it, or so he said. Mac's family seemed to own every failing eatery in the city.

"Must have been the cranberry relish," said Basil.

"Look's like pasta sauce."

"Maybe that's what it was. I don't remember."

"You don't remember lunch?"

"Not really. It was a long time ago."

Shirley felt his forehead. "I think we should see a doctor. You've been acting strangely recently. Mora and Amanda both noticed. Sangria's quite alarmed, and even Alto has his concerns."

"I'm really fine." Basil tried to sound convincing.

"Indulge me," said Shirley. "You need to see Amanda's wonderful Dr. Nasturtium while you still have full health insurance."

"No," said Basil, with surprising force. "There's nothing wrong."

"No choice," said Shirley. "I'm calling him tomorrow."

He accepted the glass of port that Shirley poured, stepped over Oscar's newest hairball and leaned back in his recliner. What had he eaten at Buster's Gourmet Souse Café? Souse and cranberry? Souse in wine sauce? Souse in catsup? That was more like it. Buster had said they needed reservations even though the place was empty. "It fills up fast," Mac added knowingly. Basil had never liked the idea of souse as a child, and remembered avoiding it as an adult at a charity function with Shirley.

The buffet featured odd "delicacies" including rattlesnake burgers and moose mousse." He passed on most of the buffet's offerings until Shirley reminded him that dinner had been $75 a plate and the hostess, a member of her book club, was watching. He took a dab of souse, pretended to eat it, but spit it in his napkin then placed in his pocket. It went through the wash fairly well.

As they entered Buster's small restaurant a sign bid them to wait to be seated. Mac and Basil leaned against the door frame waiting to be called to a gold-flecked white Formica tabletop. There was a box on the wall that allowed patrons to make jukebox selections after sliding a dollar's worth of quarters in the slot. Mac borrowed four quarters from Basil and selected "You're Nothing but a Hound Dog." A gospel version.

There were two bottles of catsup and a large salt shaker in the shape of a nude woman near the napkin holder. Mac winked as he played with it.

"Buster did time, you know."

"For what?" whispered Basil.

"Don't talk about it when he's AROUND, but it had to do with . . . no, I better not say nutin." He nodded in the direction of the kitchen. Buster pushed his large frame through the double doors. He carried large platters of thick slices of souse.

Basil remembered his mother liked this, of course, and told him that he couldn't leave the table until he had finished the hunk she had deposited on his plate. "Pickled pig parts are good for you," she would say. "Head cheese," she'd breathe into his face, lifting his chin so that her look could not be misunderstood.

As a child Basil stared at the transparent gray mass on his plate until his eyes watered. He knew his mother was sitting on the other side of the kitchen door, waiting for him to choke it down. Then she'd bring some of her canned peaches, a slimy horror, for dessert, and she'd wait and wait until it was almost supper time for him to finish all of it.

Now this. In retrospect, Basil suspected that Buster had spiked his ice water with lemon with something hallucinogenic. It would have happened shortly after he had declined use of a plastic straw on environmental grounds and Buster glared at him and refilled his glass. After a few sips he felt woozy, and vaguely remembered playing with his food, making cabin walls out of pieces of souse and painting them red with catsup, perhaps using his tie as a brush. He wasn't sure where Mac had taken him after that. His eyes had been closed for most of the ride. He did remember something heavy being put in his lap, then removed at a later stop.

It wasn't clear and perhaps he had imagined it. Why would either Mac or Buster drug him? But he knew he wasn't really sick and certainly didn't need to see a doctor or get professional help, as he correctly figured Shirley was contemplating.

He sipped the port, wishing he could remember all the events of the afternoon. He recalled sirens and Mac shouting, "Duck down, they're shooting!"

And a ping as something hit the mirror on the passenger's side. And maybe another voice from the back seat asking Mac if he had a shovel and Mac saying, "Oh shit, you were 'sposed to BRING it."

And something about a tombstone or a pond. It was a blur.

The port was calming, but his mind was unsettled, like a dream that had been vivid while you're sleeping but fades in details and meaning as soon as you wake up.

Had they all been wearing ski masks? Why did Mac swear them all to secrecy if they wanted to get their full share of the moolah. The dream had turned in an alarming direction. The port slipped out of his hand and spilled on Oscar Wilde.

Basil jolted his recliner to upright, a look of horror on his face.

"What is it, dear?" asked Shirley rushing to him with her lap blanket to wipe the cat.

"Oh my God!" said Basil. "Oh dear God! No, I couldn't have!"

"What happened, darling. Tell me. You can trust me."

Basil looked at her with fear and shame. "Nothing," he said in a hoarse whisper. "Nothing happened."

How could he ever admit to Shirley what had happened, especially if he wasn't totally sure.

Shirley's voice was alarmingly soothing. "There, there," she said, wiping his brow with a damp cloth, then using it to clean the cat. "I hope the stain comes out," she said.

"My shirt?" asked Basil.

"No, from Oscar. It would be unseemly to be having kittens when you look like you have been partying all night."

"Oscar certainly partied at least once," said Basil.

"I think the babies will be here any day. Maybe tonight."

"We're taking turns sitting up with her," said Mora, who had just entered the room with Amanda.

"I've got her nest ready in her favorite dresser drawer," added Amanda. "Don't worry, Dad, it will only be for a few hours."

"My dresser? But it's my dresser. You didn't ask." He kept his eyes closed and held out his glass to Shirley for a refill.

"Oscar likes it there. It's where she'll be most comfortable. And you don't need all your sweaters at this time of year."

"I don't want kittens in my sweater drawer, or my socks drawer or my closet."

"Don't worry. We're just joking. Actually, Mora and I will pick up Oscar to take her to the office. Sangria thinks it would be a great idea to have a birthing cam set up so that the world can watch Oscar in labor, the babies popping out, then nursing. All that great stuff and then when they are toddling about, she'll let them play with the hatchlings. Kits and chicks."

Mora added, "Think of all the publicity for the company, Kenly Pope's books, and even you. The picture Amanda took of you holding baby Oscar will be in a frame next to his cage. Sangria thinks it's a great idea and we all agree."

Basil opened his eyes and stood up. "First my sweaters and now my cat. You can't do that. Oscar, as I recall, is *my* cat."

"Oh, Daddy, I don't recall that at all. You were just hanging around with us at the pet store, looking at your watch and staring at the lizards when we picked Oscar. He was so cute. Besides, you've never liked the hairballs. You don't want to be picking little baby hairballs out of your sweaters, do you?" asked Amanda

She had a point. Mora picked up Oscar and sniffed her fur. "Oscar seems to have been drinking heavily," she said. "That's not good for an expectant mother."

"It's really not what you think," said Shirley, again blotting Oscar's neck with the dish towel.

"We're taking her tomorrow," said Amanda. "She'll probably be home again about six weeks after the kittens are born. Don't worry about her. Sangria has a lovely room set up for her. The world will be watching. I think we should change her name though. Oscarina, perhaps."

Basil shook his head.

"You can watch her on TV, Dad," said Mora, "or visit her at work. She'd probably like that."

Basil looked with bewilderment at Shirley. "You knew about this? You are letting them take Oscar?"

"Well, your daughters did mention it a day or so ago. I was going to tell you at dinner, but you have seemed so preoccupied with work, or something, that the time never seemed right. Oscar will be fine. It's just for a month or so. I already have the video channel set up on our computer so we can watch her all the time."

"They are taking my cat." Basil sat back down. He could hear his mother's voice. *You can't have a cat. You won't take care of it.*

Mother was right.

10

"Feeling better?" asked Alto, when Basil stepped outside in the morning drizzle.

"Yes. I had a touch of something."

"It sure looked like you were snockered, so to speak when Mac dropped you off yesterday. Be more careful. Shall I call a cab?"

"Oh, not today." Basil looked up and down the street, hoping that Mac would not appear before he bolted to work down the sidewalk, blending with the pedestrian commuters. He ignored whatever Alto shouted after him and dodged three people on rented electric scooters, who obviously had not mastered the brakes yet.

Today, he resolved, he would be at work on time, would not leave early, and would seize the day. "Carpe diem," he said to a panhandler.

He had left earlier than usual, leaving still-snoring Shirley a note, and already missing the sound of Oscar coughing up something in the hall. Mora was living with Amanda now, so he didn't have to steer her to O.O.&O. and worry that his attempts at conversation were always taken wrong. How her view of him and the divorce were so distorted. It was obviously too late to convince her of his side of the situation with Margo the Horrible. No, just let it go without an argument. It was good to see her as an adult, and she sounds happy with her new job with Sangria. Soon he'd be done. He had decided that working for Mac might not be the best temporary job. There were all kinds of volunteer or part-time options to pursue. What they were, he wasn't sure, but he'd have time soon to leisurely start his day, and by golly it wouldn't be with tofu eggs! No, he would seize the day where it came to food too.

never used your petty cash fund so he was able to provide drinks and dessert as well."

Basil tried to nod enthusiastically as he sneezed several times. "Darwin's done a fine job," he sniffed.

"I think so too," said Sangria. "I've made another decision. An important one, Basil." She looked hard at him and tossed a box of tissues in his direction. "Stop that sniffling."

He couldn't.

She continued. "I plan to delay your retirement, which I can because you had objected to the retirement date early on. Now you can help with the book launch and see that your staff will give Kenly's two new books the proper go-over so we can, and I realize this is indelicate . . . so we need to crank them out. Big money in this sort of thing."

Mora and Amanda beamed.

Basil rolled back his chair as Cleopatra flounced near his space. His eyes watered. He felt weak. Sangria couldn't mean he would have to stay longer. He had the right to retire, didn't he? Or would he lose his benefits if he didn't agree to stay? This had to be a case of age discrimination or the reverse of it. His brain felt feathery. He tried to focus. Darwin was providing the marketing team with what he called the brilliant essences of the book for back cover blurbs to quote. He said he had to make only minor suggestions, but loved the ending, and how it led perfectly into a sequel with Ash and Dresden stepping out of their ranch in the hills of North Dakota to the sound of gunfire.

Sangria said, "Yes, oh yes. Basil, I hope you've put in for a hefty raise for this fine young man."

Basil looked at the fine young man through his watery eyes, wishing he had never been talked into hiring him. He had never liked the obsequious little bastard less than this moment. But perhaps he could talk Sangria into promoting Darwin into his own position. Let him be editor. That would teach him to promote a stupid book. Basil realized he was not using his words, he words befitting the editor of a major, or at least once major, publishing house. "Obsequious" was good, but not "bastard" or "stupid." He would have changed those if he had seen them in a text.

"Basil, are you listening?" Sangria's voice had a familiar edge.

"Yes."

"Then, you'll take care of it."

"Of what?" He knew he was in trouble by the sudden silence at the table.

"Darwin," whispered Amanda.

"Oh, yes, Darwin." Basil was relieved. Of course he would go this very afternoon to human resources and request a five percent raise, maybe even ten percent, for this wonderful, hardworking staffer. In fact, he'd do it right now.

"On my way," said Basil. "I'm on my way." He saw a rare smile flicker across Darwin's face.

Of course it wasn't that easy. Eugene Hodgkins, personnel director, told Basil that he needed a performance evaluation filled out and signed by Sangria. Because none had ever been done, Basil would have to reconstruct Darwin's work since he had been hired, and Basil and Darwin would need to discuss each evaluation separately, and both would have to sign the paperwork. So on and so forth. And then Basil, as manager of the editing department would need to calculate what sort of raise Darwin would have received all those many years, minus the two years that there were no raises (although ten-pound turkeys had been given to all employees at Christmas) total the amounts and check with accounting about how much was available, with interest, for Darwin. When Basil said he hadn't received much of a raise himself in that period of time, Hodgkins said, "You don't want to go there."

Armed with a pad of evaluation forms in triplicate for the first few years of Darwin's career and with instructions on how to fill out the forms online after that (when the company had switched to paperless forms), Basil returned to the office. Darwin looked up hopefully.

"We have things to do," said Basil, trying to figure out what they were.

"Since you know better than I what you've been doing all this time, I'd like you to fill out these forms, one for each year. Be sure to put in a good word for yourself." He placed the papers and computer instructions on Darwin's desk next to the spinner.

"Yes, sir," he said.

Basil returned to his office and began righting the warthogs. Even their grinning babies with tusks snapped off, and new variously sized hostile ones he didn't recognize—were now involved in risque behaviors. The largest ones seemed to be preparing for an uprising. Against who? Against him? Or something else? He trembled. Those responsible for this behavior had gone too far. He studied the collection and knew that it was time to try to seize the day.

11

"What's that?" asked Shirley suspiciously. She stirred the pot of sauce for her gluten-free pasta with gluten-free extra vegetable sauce.

"Momo, my surprise," said Mora. "Try it." She placed a covered casserole dish on the counter.

"She won't tell me what's in it," said Amanda, "and she wouldn't let me in the kitchen while she was cooking."

"You promised to have some," said Mora.

"Vegans don't eat some things, as you know," said Amanda.

"You did promise. You've only been a full vegan for a few months, a lapsed one as recently as yesterday when we had ice cream—double chocolate with whipped cream."

"No," said Shirley, shocked. "You didn't."

Amanda's face flushed. "Okay, I'll try a bite."

Basil was even more suspicious of the little dumplings when the dish was passed. But his daughters were watching his spoon dip in once, then a second time.

Amanda and Shirley each selected one and Mora started with three momos.

"Ready, set, taste," said Mora with a grin.

Basil rolled the dumpling on his tongue before biting in with a startled *umpff*. He couldn't tell if he liked it or not.

Always the pleaser, Amanda said they were quite yummy, a word she rarely used with her vegan frozen dinners, and Shirley tried to be polite and pleasant as she picked away at hers.

"Now tell us, Mora, dear, about your ingredients."

Mora thought for a moment then said, "Well, they weren't easy to obtain. Momo is something we ate a lot over there. And I'm glad you all love it. It is made with yak, stewed or ground. Next we have yak milk and butter stirred into fermented tea, and yak cheese that is eaten either crunchy or dried. My favorite way to cook it is slowly so that it oozes with the spicy green chilies."

"Oh my!" said Shirley. "You're not serving fermented tea, are you dear?"

"You have to try it at least once," said Mora. "I realize my life has been more adventurous than you're used to, but you may travel one day when Dad retires."

Basil cleared his throat. "Actually, I'm impressed with the rather unusual flavor and textures of the momo. I think this would be a fine dish to serve at a staff meeting. Sangria has Potluck Fridays once a month." He covered his mouth with a napkin to hide his smile. "There's always a lot of yakety-yak at those lunches anyway."

"Basil, do you really think that's appropriate?" asked Shirley as she tried to hide the last bit of momo under her napkin.

"It would be perfect," said Basil. "I will pay for the special ingredients."

"Dad, are you feeling well?" asked Amanda.

"Never better," said Basil. "Carpe diem." He excused himself. The house seem oddly off. Then he realized why. There were no hairballs in his path to his recliner. He didn't like Oscar but he missed him. He was annoyed that Sangria had imposed visiting hours as Oscar's due date neared. He had every right to see his cat, but Oscar was cloistered in a section of Sangria's office that he had heard from the interns was labeled FELINE MATERNITY. If he did insist on going in, the feathers would be a problem. Perhaps he could persuade Mora to arrange a visitation outside Sangria's office—in the men's room perhaps. He poured an after-yak-Cabernet and washed down the momo's aftertaste.

Two more dreadful books by Kenly Pope before he could make his exit. But what if Pope wanted to write like the drivel after drivel of best-selling novelists. Their books are eventually ghostwritten with a name added to the cover. Fans were happy. The publisher was happy. That was what it was all about. If he were ever to write a book, he probably couldn't even get it looked at by the Ozzies or any other house. He could title it *Sadsack,* or *Revenge of the Warthogs.* That might be catchier. Titles matter. It might be a fictionalized version of his life. Or maybe a mystery—the unsolved murder of a first wife. *Killer Sonata,* might work.

That could be the first in a best-selling series. *Last Sangria. Mac the Scalpel. Feathered Enemies. The Cat Thief. Murder in the Board Room. Die Chickens Die!*

He could hear his family cleaning up. Occasionally, his name was mentioned and then the conversation was quieter. It didn't matter. He had no curiosity about their worries. They had no idea what had been going on in his life in recent weeks, which was just as well.

He would ask for, no demand, the first pick of Oscar's litter, would not allow his kitten to live with the Ozzies and would never again complain about hairballs or where it slept. In fact, he would be pleased to have it hang out next to his typewriter when he worked on his best seller in retirement. He didn't hear Mora and Amanda leave, nor Shirley tiptoe into her room to work on her Christmas craft project that involved stringing aluminum pop tabs; Alto seemed to have an endless supply of the aluminum rings and suggestions of where she could donate or sell her crafts.

The phone jarred Basil awake from his Cabernet-induced doze. The muffled voice of the unfamiliar stranger on the other end of the line gave him shivers. "If you know what's good for you, you'll take the cab waiting in front of the building. Now."

"Don't threaten me," said Basil, forcefully.

"Why not? We got business to take care of."

"No we don't. I'm not coming down."

"Didn't you see the paper's front-page story and your description? Don't you want your share of the moolah or shall I drop it off at the police department? The bank bag has your name on it."

Basil was more than shivering. He was shaking and sweating.

"I had nothing to do with that," he mustered.

"Oh, yeah? So you had nothing to do with it but ya know exactly what I'm talking about. Sleeping through something doesn't mean you can't be charged wit participating."

"Someone drugged me."

"That's what they all say. Are you coming down or not?"

"Absolutely not! I don't want the money. I'm not involved. I don't want to talk with you."

The caller did not respond.

"Basil, who's that calling at this hour," asked Shirley from her craft room.

"Nothing important dear. I forgot something . . . uh . . . at the office and I need to go get it. Be right back," he responded.

"Who ya talking wit?" asked the voice.

"My wife. Leave her out of this. I'll be right down."

He slipped into his loafers and warm jacket. Nervous perspiration seeped into a cap that Amanda had made for him before she rejected all animal fibers. He wished it wasn't so colorful. He headed out.

"Don't be late," called Shirley. "I don't want to call the cops."

He heard her laugh gaily as he shut the door.

Alto, working a late shift, opened the door and said, "Good luck," rather ominously. The doorman, his breath heavy with mint, pointed at a cab. Basil was relieved that it didn't look like Mac's usual vehicle, a dull black late 1989 Spirit. This older one was dented in a number of places and the windshield had cracks. The cab inched forward and Alto opened the door to the backseat, glanced at the driver and waved Basil inside.

Mac. Buster.

Basil tried to open the door, but it had locked when the cab lurched forward.

"Excuse me," Basil said, "I really can't go out tonight. Shirley is expecting me to, uh, help her with the dishes and then we're going to watch 'Law and Order.' It's our favorite show, you know about how the good guys *always* catch the bad guys." When there was no response, Basil continued. "Then we watch reruns of 'NCIS,' and 'Superman.' 'Batman' sometimes. Bad guys never win."

Basil looked out the window trying to figure out where they were and where they were going so that he could find his way home if he ever had the opportunity to escape whatever they had planned. The streets grew darker and darker as they left the city and turned north on Rte. 129. It had been a long time since he had traveled this highway. Perhaps the last time was when Amanda was in junior high. Shirley thought it would be just lovely if the three of them had a weekend at the shore in a cozy cabin, with a view of the ocean, that she had rented for Labor Day weekend. Amanda couldn't imagine going off with her parents, so Shirley relented and allowed the teen to bring two of her friends. It was also the weekend of the a rare marital fight. Basil couldn't remember exactly what had started it but as he now recalled, it had something to do with a burned omelet. Or was it burned oatmeal? Something with an O. Or maybe it was over the Ozzies, who had announced they were changing the staff's benefits to favor new hires over those that had been there for more than fifteen years. Maybe he had thrown the omelet at Shirley after she said she was unhappy but could understand the Ozzies' logic.

"The logic of what?" he had yelled. "I should be getting a big raise this year and more time off." He turned the omelet over in the skillet.

"Think of all those people just starting at the bottom."

"I just started at the bottom too, and had to work my way up."

Don't raise your voice," she said loudly.

That's when his scorched, special-occasion, well-aimed mushroom, cheese, onion and pepper omelet flipped across the room and slapped the kitchen window that overlooked the beach where Amanda and her friends were applying baby oil to enhance their tans.

Without staying to clean up the mess, Basil, still wearing his pajamas, stomped out to water's edge and waded waist deep. He floated for a while, ignoring Shirley's shouts from the dunes. He rarely lost his temper with her, but this ongoing defense of the indefensible at his job had reached its limits. She should be on his side. Let her be mad about the omelet.

The shouts were louder, sounding like a crowd was involved, and then whistles. It suddenly dawned on him what they were saying. He looked around and saw the fins.

Would Mac and Buster be taking him to the beach? To throw him to the sharks?

"Could I ask where we're going?" Basil asked politely.

"You could," said Buster, "but you'll remember when we get there."

The cab took a right at exit 87 and after about five minutes, another right on a poorly paved road that went through cemetery gates.

"Oh, no," moaned Basil.

The cab passed a number of tombstones barely visible in the dark, then stopped next to a very recent grave. A fresh mound of dirt was sprinkled with grass seed. Mac and Buster got out. Basil could hear them open the cab's trunk.

"Open YOUR door," said Mac. "Stop looking so worked up." He handed Basil a shovel, and another to Buster.

"Dig," said Mac.

Basil took small scoops and placed them neatly to the side.

"Dig," repeated Mac. "Dig like Buster."

Buster's shoveling reminded Basil of how Alfred's beagle had excavated great holes in his friend's yard. Wild sprays of dirt disappeared into the lawn so that the holes could never be refilled by what had been removed.

Their shovels simultaneously struck something hard about four feet beneath the surface.

Buster grunted when Mac directed them to go into the hole and lift the box out.

"You do sometin," said Buster.

"I'm the lookout," was Mac's reply.

Basil thought of running, but where? He was too tall to hide behind the gravestones, and he was in dangerous company if cops caught up with him.

He slid in a cascade of crumbled soil to the bottom and helped Buster lift the box, the size, he guessed, of a toddler's coffin.

Mac handed Basil a crow bar and told him to pop off the top. He shone his flashlight inside and said, "Damn!" He threw his cap on the ground and cursed again.

"They GOT to it. They took it. Damn!"

"Took what?" asked Basil.

"You know what. You were here with us. They were watching, or were you? Did you come back on your own yesterday? Wuz it you Basil, sweetheart? I trusted you with my barber tools at the zoo and then you steal our stuff?" He leaned back against the cab and glared.

"Never, never, never! I swear I don't remember coming here or leaving here or anything at any time. I don't know anything. Really. Someone drugged me. At least I think that's what happened."

Mac scowled thoughtfully. "If not you, THEN who? Who would take our money and leave a kid?"

"A dead child? We dug up someone's grave?" Basil sunk to his knees.

"Nah, the goat kind with a bell around its neck. Look's like it was embalmed. People are like that with their pets. Look here, a note says, 'Love forever, Nanny.'"

Buster coughed. "Mac, maybe we dug in the wrong spot. But we better go. Here comes lights."

"Fill the hole fast," barked Mac. He cupped clods of dirt and hurled them on the hastily lowered coffin.

"Too late," said Basil, as two squad cars pulled up. An officer got out and called in the license on the cab. Another asked for identification, a third asked for an explanation. Basil had none.

Mac said they were suffering from terrible grief at the loss of the kid and they just wanted to say good-bye one more time.

Buster wiped his eyes and muttered, "Amen."

"Let's have a look," said the second officer. "We've had reports of thieves burying stolen goods and cash back here in this old cemetery."

"That's terrible," said Mac. "Stuff like that goes ON in a sacred place? Maybe we should remove little Jesse's coffin and place it in someplace safe. Would you help us, officer? Basil's sister would be so grateful." He nodded in Basil's direction.

The speaker in the police car crackled with information. The first officer said, "Cab comes back to a MacCabbie company. He's legit."

"Sorry for your loss, sir," the officer said to Basil. "Do you want the box in the back of the cab?" They helped retrieve the partially buried coffin.

"Yes, sir," said Mac. "We'll find a new SPOT tomorrow. Hope you locate the crooks who are disturbing this beautiful site. Just not right."

With the coffin carefully placed on the seat next to Basil, the police drove off and Mac and Buster returned to their seats in the front.

"What now?" asked Buster. "Do we wait till they go away and dig some more."

"Nah, not tonight. We just gotta get rid of this box. Whaddya think, Basil? Find a bridge and splash it?"

Basil felt surprisingly coherent. "The cops have your name. If the people come back to visit the kid's grave they'll see the box is gone and the cops will know you had it. We should rebury it."

"They won't come back. It's illegal to bury animals in a people cemetery. Your nephew, Jesse, should have been in the pet cemetery. Let's go."

"Let me out," said Basil through clenched teeth. "He's not my nephew. Now!"

As he reached for the door, child locks clicked.

"Besides, Jesse has a cute beard that needs trimming," said Mac.

Alto opened the door when they reached Basil's apartment building. "Let me help you lift this," he said, reaching for the wooden box

"Oh, well, this isn't mine," whispered Basil. He quickly pushed the box away from him and moved his feet toward the curb.

"Hold it right there, Baz," said Mac. "My COMPANY can't be responsible for packages that are left behind. Especially, a nice expensive anniversary gift for your lovely wife, Shirley. You wouldn't want us to spoil the surprise, wouldja?"

"You wouldn't tell Shirley!"

"Just kidding, if you know what I mean," said Mac. "But hurry along with the present. We gotta go."

Alto helped Basil out of the car and opened the main door to the lobby.

Basil stopped just inside. "Alto, I'm wondering if there's a storage area where I can keep this box for now."

Alto studied it. "The box looks like a coffin. What kinda gift did you get her?"

Basil hoped he would sound convincing. "Shirley has always wanted a big jewelry box. She saw one on the Internet. Um, it can hold all her other jewelry boxes so in case there is a fire or earthquake, she can grab it and take everything with her."

"Makes sense, I guess," said Alto, "but it's kinda heavy and I hear a tinkly sound."

"Uh, that's because I already got her a charm bracelet with lots of little bells. You know how women like bangly things."

Alto nodded, but mumbled that he didn't know because his wife just had tattoos. "I'll take care of it." He walked to a locked storeroom next to the elevator and placed the casket on the bottom shelf.

Basil quietly opened the door to his apartment, hoping Shirley was sleeping. She was not. Her eyes were red. "And where have you been?"

"Uh, shopping."

"At this hour of the night? For what? For whom? Some tawdry office worker? The one who calls and hangs up after leaving a strange message that probably sets up a tryst with you?"

Basil slipped out of his shoes, wishing for the distraction of Oscar Wilde's deposits on the carpet.

"Shirley dear, there is no tawdry office worker in my life. I was, uh, shopping for you, for our anniversary."

"Nonsense," said Shirley. "You've never done that before. And just when do you think that our anniversary is that you would go on this errand until one A.M.?"

"Tomorrow?" asked Basil.

"Ha! It's seven months from now."

"Just wanted to be ready this year."

Shirley glared. "There's a message next to the phone. A woman. Her message was in code." She sniffled, and locked the guest bedroom door behind her.

Who could be calling him without leaving a message? What tawdry or not office worker? Certainly not Mrs. Joyce Royce! Bunny would never call his home. Basil trembled.

Basil picked up the note Shirley had transcribed: "Take the flower from the thorns."

It made no sense. Shirley must have misunderstood.

But Shirley hadn't been mistaken, as Basil learned when he arrived at his office. The same direction was written on a sticky note affixed to his door. Sangria's handwriting.

He took it to Darwin for translation. Darwin wiped his glasses on his shirt and solemnly studied the note.

"Ah, this is a new linguistic substitute for people who want to get rid of anti-animal sayings. If you wanted someone to get busy, take charge, and do something, what would you normally say in the anti-animal vernacular?"

"I would say, 'Get busy, take charge, and do something,'" said Basil.

Darwin said, "Well, boss, I've heard you say, 'Take the bull by the horns.'"

"What's wrong with that?"

"It's anti-animal. Think of the poor bull."

"I will think of the poor bull when I order my next steak," said Basil. "This is nonsense."

"Not to Sangria. If you are not careful in her company, you may be led like a lamb led to the slaughter," cautioned Darwin. "She's pushing to take the flowers by the thorns, and your fingers, sir, may get pricked in the process, if you know what I mean."

"I don't know what you mean, but it doesn't matter." Basil went back into his office and stared at the warthogs. A faint smile tugged at Darwin's lips. He was very pleased that Sangria had adopted his suggestion.

Basil rearranged the warthogs in family friendly positions and noticed a new one to the left of the biggest sounders. A large sow with lovely eyelashes appeared to be wanting to join the other females and three boars were headed in her direction. A tiny red bow had been tied to her right tusk that curled suggestively above her lips. Its toes glowed with gold paint.

Basil fingered the tusk. Could it be real ivory? Not unless it had been smuggled or was an antique that owners had been cautioned to claim was made from "bone." Where had it come from? Who would have given him such a special gift? Surely not his Shirley.

Warthogs and Feathers

His intercom buzzed then crackled with Sangria's voice. "Meeting in my office in five minutes. In case you're wondering what it's about, you'll just have to guess. Curiosity thrilled the cat."

What cat? Oscar Wilde perhaps? He/she couldn't be thrilled by detention in Sangria's growing menagerie. Basil would pay him a visit today. But meanwhile, should he leave the new warthog with the others or place her in a special safe place? The interns might damage her when they did their constant rearrangements while he was out. He looked around his room. Other than his credenza where the other warthogs roamed, he only had his large desk with its heavy wooden drawers. He slipped the warthog, which he had silently named "Honey," in the pocket of his suit jacket and hung the coat on a rack. He sprayed his nostrils with antihistamine, donned a face mask, and headed for the elevator.

"My first egg," announced Sangria. She handed it to Darwin, whose chair was surprisingly close to her desk. *And a new pecking order*, thought Basil, amused at his wit, but concerned about what this could mean.

Darwin rolled it in his palm and exclaimed about its texture and chocolate hue. Basil was about to ask if it was edible but realized that would be a grave error. He looked around, wondering where Oscar Wilde was penned.

"Now, Darwin, you may have the honor of placing it in the incubator," said Sangria. The young man's pimples glowed as he stepped over to the incubator and carefully placed the egg inside.

Through his mask, Basil asked why Cleo wasn't allowed to take care of the egg. Sangria stroked the hen. "She's too busy, that's why. The media will return to film the egg. Hatch Day will dominate the six o'clock news, right Darwin?"

"Yes, ma'am," said Darwin. He handed Cleo some organic chicken feed he had brought as a treat.

"May I go now?" asked Basil. His efforts to stand from a rolling office chair caused Cleo to flap to the top of a bookcase.

"Look what you did!" said Sangria.

"I'll get her," said Darwin. "Come to Uncle Darwin, sweetie." The hen cocked her head and hopped down to his arm.

posture and facial expression his former interns, including Darwin, had assumed when he called them in for a meeting. A look of attention masking a mind wandering to personal issues. His personal issues involved 1. Finding and freeing Oscar and Honey the Warthog; 2, resigning; 3, assuming a new identity, perhaps in a foreign country, or in an occupation where he would not be identified. He would not tell Shirley, Amanda or Mora. They had stopped caring about him when they took up with his nemesis, Sangria. 4. He would eat nothing but meat every meal.

He would disappear. The *Times* might have a brief about a former chief editor of a longtime publishing house that had mysteriously vanished. Who would really care in this age of downsizing? There would be talk on the street, in the publishing world. Maybe speculation in *Publisher's Weekly* about a kidnapping of a prominent book editor. Then he would be forgotten in the new hype for Kenly Pope's books. And, he hoped that he would learn about a mysterious case of poultry flu that had taken the life, untimely of course, of Sangria Ozburn. He would know of all these things from watching a television at bar in Jamaica or in Tiajuana, where he had let his beard grow while making tortillas.

"So, you'll have a draft ready on Thursday?" asked Darwin.

Basil nodded, a firmness in his jaw that he didn't realize was possible. He looked at his legal pad where he had jotted: Need help to rescue Oscar.

He sensed that Darwin was watching him stumble toward his temporary desk where the intern had been sitting until that morning. He knew that the other interns in the room were no longer pretending to work but had turned to watch this humiliating moment. Basil ignored them. He also ignored the papers and instructions that Darwin had left on the desk for him. He needed to find a safe place for the warthogs. Basil opened the top drawer of the desk. Cleaned out. Not even a spinner. So were all the other metal drawers. Files had been emptied. It appeared that Darwin had planned more than a temporary move.

"Go back to work," Basil said to the staff.

No one said anything and none followed his order. *Let Darwin deal with them,* Basil thought. It was a liberating moment. Basil folded his hands, then pushed the stack of papers to one side. The company become derailed when Sangria became the third partner. No, it was before that. OMO wasn't a very good influence, but at least he knew the business and people wanted to learn and work. There was process and performance. Decent authors. Decent editors. Terrific editors, like himself. Respected editors and bosses. OMO was the very model, even if it was old-fashioned. And what is wrong with old-fashioned when it's better than new-fashioned?

He worried about the safety of Honey. She had barely had time to become familiar with the rest of the sounders when his demotion happened, and he was sure that was what this sudden coup by Darwin was all about. All these months he had been trying to help the nerd, yet the creep had been plotting to take his job just because he hadn't put in for a raise for him or given him enough to do.

And then there was Shirley and the daughters. Shirley, who had loved his sonatas. Shirley who rubbed his feet and poured his port, fixed fragrant pot roasts and almost never fussed when he cursed about Oscar's hairballs. But now she had support: Amanda and Mora in their strange and new food choices and in their hasty snatching of his cat. Worse, they had become buddies with Sangria the Terrible, who won't let him retire.

He had to come up with a plan. Fast.

Basil would show them all. He needed Mac. Mac had offered him a job. Mac would help him rescue Oscar. Mac could hide him out. Mac had money. Maybe lots of money. Maybe he had lots of money too. Mac had flaws. Dangerous flaws, but he knew how to seize the day with crazy adventures. Basil escaped boredom in that cab and was living on the edge. There was a certain allure to that.

He realized that he had better pretend to work like the rest of the interns. He could see that Sydney was playing Solitaire on his computer; Nadia was whispering into a cell phone hidden just below the neckline of her sweater and Moris (with one R) was texting. Morris (with two Rs) was playing Words with Friends.

Basil wondered when he could take a lunch break—an extended one, perhaps.

He looked at Darwin, who was staring at him, smiled and picked up his red pen and waved it at his former subordinate. Basil had to make his plan, but until then, he would be civil. Even obsequious.

12

Shirley did not have drinky-poos ready. She was not waiting for Basil in their family room. The fragrance of a homemade meal, vegan or otherwise, did not fill the area. She sat at the kitchen table with an upended wastebasket in front of her and piles of torn envelopes and letters. His.

"That's my trash," Basil said. "What are you doing?"

Shirley's voice had an unaccustomed edge. "Looking for evidence."

"Of what?" He was genuinely baffled.

"Oh, don't sound so innocent. The other women. I thought perhaps there might have been a note or card. Some cryptic message. Our daughters have permission from Sangria to search your computer files."

Basil cleared his throat. He couldn't think of a response. It was so absurd.

Shirley continued, choking back a sob. "And don't try to tell me otherwise. You've been leaving work and not returning. Acting strangely. Not getting your work done. Don't you think I know that the wife is the last to know?"

"I can explain," said Basil, but he wasn't sure he could.

"Don't bother," said Shirley. "I have engaged a private investigator."

"A what?"

"Highly recommended through Alto. And it will all come out in court." She swept most of the trash back into the basket with a grand wave of her right arm.

"Alto? The doorman?"

"He knows more than you think," said Shirley. "And he's about to tell."

"This is all a mistake, I swear. How can I prove it?" He took a large step toward her.

"Stay back. I'm in no mood. This is been one of the top three most awful days of my life. The first was telling you that I liked your sonatas. The second was meeting your mother, and now this betrayal."

"Shirley, but what about us? We love each other. We have daughters, and a cat and I'm going to retire soon and take up, uh, whatever you want me to do, and we'll live wherever you want to live."

"I don't know if I can trust you ever again. Make your own supper. I'm going to dine with our daughters and I may spend the night with them."

"Shirley, don't leave me alone. We need to talk. I know I have been behaving . . . I've been having problems lately, mostly at work."

She crossed her arms and stared. "Go on."

"Things have been rocky since Sangria joined the firm."

"We all like her."

"You aren't me," said Basil. He pulled out a chair from across the table and sat. He wished Shirley had something other than ripped envelopes on the table. He couldn't remember when he had last eaten.

"I have no authority, no respect with my staff anymore," said Basil, lowering his head.

"Go on."

"Sangria has chickens in her office. I'm allergic."

"Go on."

"I lost my wallet."

"Again?"

"No, but things still aren't straightened out and I'm supposed to work on marketing a terrible book."

"Terrible? Who wrote it?"

"Kenly Pope. I think he's a friend of Sangria's."

He looked up. Shirley was scowling. "What's wrong with the book?"

"The plot and characters."

"That's rather judgemental of you," said Shirley. "You probably think that on principle that a book by an unknown author is no good."

"It's my job, or was my job, to be judgemental. I'm the chief editor, or used to be. And I'm not allowed to retire as announced. Do you understand now why I've been out of sorts?" He looked pleadingly at his wife. Why didn't she understand? Why wasn't she jumping to her feet and rushing over to comfort him?

"That's not the entire story," said Shirley.

Basil blinked.

"My sources say that you leave many afternoons with persons unknown to me and places unknown. You've been seen at the zoo. You never liked the zoo. I tried to get you to take Amanda to the zoo when she was six, but you said the zoo made you sneeze."

"That was different," said Basil, unable to remember that he had denied little Amanda that experience.

"You've been sneaking off. What am I to assume? What would any wife assume? Well, I can only continue to assume you are seeing another woman." She slammed her hand on the table.

Basil blinked. His voice quavered. "Not true. We were never . . ." No, that wasn't the right thing to say, but it was too late.

"Just as I suspected," said Shirley. "Alto said he'd call a cab, and I'm ready." She angrily pushed her chair back and picked up her travel carry-on that Basil hadn't noticed.

"My lawyer will be in touch," she said.

Basil didn't get up. His muscles had no memory of what muscles to move. He had never thought that Shirley, dear Shirley, would treat him like this. She was behaving more like Margo. Cold, mistrustful Margo, who hated his sonatas and accused him of having an affair with Shirley, even though she didn't know her name at the time.

He wouldn't admit it to Margo, but Shirley was warm and encouraging. She touched his arm, fixed him drinky-poos, and sat next to him on the piano bench while he played for her. She was impressed with his job at the publishing company.

Margo told him he wouldn't amount to anything in a family-owned business. "They will screw you in the end," she said coldly. "You have no future in music, either," she added. "So you better find something that pays well that we can count on."

He was glad to see Margo leave, but wished she hadn't taken little Mora with her. Mora, the strange, solemn child he never really knew. Margo always had her tucked in before he got home from his long days at work and told him not to bother the child. He couldn't say he had missed Mora all the years she and her mother were living overseas. He had never really known her.

He would not let that happen again while Amanda was growing up. He read her first-edition author-signed books from the children's division. But he couldn't get time off to go to her school plays or birthday parties. He had always worked hard for the family, and Shirley and Amanda seemed happy. And he had occasionally composed a new sonata dedicated to his wife and daughter, although in his mind, one particularly lovely piece in E-flat, was to Mrs. Joyce Royce. He had never told her. She didn't have a piano and only listened to country music. He called it Sonata No. 25 (Country Memories) and dedicated it to Shirley and Amanda.

Basil had a sudden yearning to play the piece, but first made a gluten-free bread sandwich with nut spread. He poured a tall port to wash it down, and headed for his piano, not caring if he would bother the new tenants below. The country sonata had some forte moments, as he recalled.

He was only a few measures into the opening adagio, when the phone rang. He was going to ignore it but when the answering machine picked up he could hear Mac's voice. "Pick up, buddy. I know you're up there."

Basil sighed and answered. "Hello."

Mac said, "Buzz me in. We got stuff to talk about."

"It's night," said Basil.

"Youse think I don't know that? I know youse alone 'cause I just drove your beautiful former wife to your daughters' place. Ex sounds done."

Basil hit the buzzer.

Mac entered and quickly settled in Shirley's recliner. "Whatcha drinking?"

"Aren't you still on duty?" asked Basil.

"Don't matter, my cousin is on patrol tonight. Look, I came by to help you. Alto says something is wrong and I've got experience in matters like these."

Basil gave Mac a beer and topped off his glass. He rubbed his temples and closed his eyes, waiting for Mac to start, but Mac was unnaturally silent. "So, what's going on," Basil ventured.

"I gotta hand it to you," said Mac. "You didn't spill the beans with the Ex. You took the lumps for our team by admitting to the other woman affair."

"I never admitted that or anything else."

"But your Ex filled in the blanks and well, I had to agree with her."

"You didn't! How dare you!" shouted Basil, imagining rubbing a platter of tofu in the cabbie's face.

"Think of the positive, Baz. With the Ex out, we can use this apartment as our base. No one will suspect us here."

Basil rose to his feet and towered over Mac. "Never. Never. Never! I'm done with crime and your buddies. Done. Get out and don't ever contact me again. Out!"

Mac kicked up the recliner's foot rest and leaned back. He tapped his fingers on the soft armrest staining the rosy faux leather with his greasy fingers.

"Get your dirty fingers out of my apartment before Shirley comes back."

"Baz, that's not going to happen, and in five minutes you will hear Alto buzz you and the boys will be here. You can figure out where they will be sleeping. Might even want your bed now that the cat's gone."

"I'm calling the police," said Baz.

"And what would you tell them that they would believe?"

Basil slumped back in his chair. Mac was right. They would remember him barefoot, in his pajamas out on the street, finally releasing him to Shirley's custody. They would recognize him from sitting in Mac's cab with an illegal street vendor. Hadn't he been stopped other times? Was there security footage of him at the zoo? How could his life been so upended? He had never been in trouble in second grade or participated in senior pranks. He had excelled in college English. He had provided for both wives and daughters. Prepared a dutiful, albeit dishonest, eulogy at his mother's funeral. Why had he said she was a loving mother? He had been totally private about his—how should he categorize it?—secret lust for Mrs. Joyce Royce, at least until that happenstance meeting in the subway. Bunny confessed her longtime affection for him. Was that so wrong to be invited to her apartment? At his age? With his life gone so amok? And why had he lost his grip? He had no control over his staff, his wife, daughters, cat and especially now Mac. This is not how Basil had ever anticipated his golden years unfolding. He couldn't seize the moment let alone the day. He missed Oscar Wilde.

The buzzer sounded again. Mac went to the keypad next to the front door and pressed enter. Soon there was pounding on the stairs and a knock—three times—on the door. Mac opened it just a crack. "What's the password?"

"Hernando's Hideway."

"Wipe your shoes and take them off," Mac ordered the three men.

Basil didn't want to see who was there. He knew they had to be more cousins, uncles or other relations.

Mac was busy telling the men where to put their bags and showing them around the house. "Pizza in the kitchen," he said. "Don't make mess. Our host is a prude. A neatnick who collects warthogs." Basil didn't like the sarcasm, especially about wiping their shoes. Shirley would have a fit when she saw the mud on her carpet.

"Who's the guy with the long neck in that chair?" asked one.

"Basil. Baz," said Mac. "We gotta get him a NEW identity, now that he's one of us."

"How about Herb," said another. "Isn't basil a herb?"

No one laughed but Mac said, "That'll do. So, Herbie, you can open your eyes and meet your new guests. We'll be staying UNTIL the coast is clear."

Basil did not respond. There was no point. At least not yet.

He sprang to life when he heard one of Mac's gang banging out a few notes on the piano.

"Thunder and rain," said the man laughing as he pounded on the lower keys then made the upper ones tinkle.

Warthogs and Feathers

"Away from my piano!" shouted Basil, pushing the man aside.

"No roughing anyone up, Herbie," warned Mac.

"It's my piano. Mine."

"Then play for us," said Mac. "We like entertainment during our MEAL."

Basil hesitated, then realized he had nothing to lose.

He sat on the round piano stool that swivelled. How little Mora liked to spin on it. His hands hovered gracefully over the chords, then dropped like swallows onto the keys and he began the adagio from the beginning's plaintive notes. His third sonata. The key of D#. He was aware of steps coming from the kitchen. He heard chewing with mouths open behind him. Breath, rancid against his ear. Something cold and sharp on his cheek. A whisper. "Stop right now. We didn't mean that you should play something like that. Play Sinatra. Play 'When the Moon hits the Sky like a Big Pizza Pie.' Play 'Danny Boy.'"

"I don't have the music," said Basil.

"Then GO to the store and get some," said Mac.

"It's dark and the store is closed."

"Not a problem for my boys," said Mac. "And you're going with them."

"No."

"Yes, Herb. You need to PROVE yourself."

Basil felt courage, like bile, rising in his throat. He would prove himself, all right, but not in the way they expected. He dropped the curved cover over the keyboard and slowly spun toward Mac. "I will not. I am not a crook. I don't care what Shirley or the cops believe. I'm done. Done. There are limits and this crosses the line. I will not, I repeat, steal music."

His fingers trembled. He forced himself to raise his head and stare at Mac. The barber's eyes glinted like the razor blade he now brandished.

"So kill me," said Basil calmly. "There will be a struggle, of course, and the cops will know I put up a fight and I will be totally exonerated."

He could see that Mac was considering this possibility. His buddies had backed off and were seated with their feet on Shirley's antique coffee table.

"And put your dirty feet on the floor," said Basil with a firmness he hadn't been able to summon since Mora's mother had grabbed the child's hand and slammed the door. "And don't come back," Basil shouted.

His inner warthog had taken over and was itching for battle.

Mac slid the sheath over the blade and stroked his sideburns. "You, know, Baz, we go back a LONG way, you and me, and I don't like your tone. I've been trying to help you. You got problems. Big problems. And do you have friends? Do you have family that cares? Do you know what you will do when you get fired? Uh-huh, that could happen after all the trouble you've been in. There's only one person you can depend on and that's me. Mac. I've offered you jobs and despite your refusal to go with the boys tonight, I'm ready to forgive. I have a big heart. Alto has a big heart. My boys have a big heart. We're not going to leave you in your time of need. In fact, while we make ourselves at home, I will personally drop you off at that hanky-panky's house."

Basil's face reddened. His courage now filled his bladder. "I have to pee," he whispered.

"Take your time," said Mac. "We'll be waiting."

Basil needed time. He locked the bathroom door. He struggled with his zipper. Nothing seemed to be working. He leaned his head against the window, and raised it for fresh air. Below was a small ledge and a fire escape ladder that dropped to the alley. He hadn't paid attention to it before.

There was a light knock on the door. "Done yet, Baz?"

"No. Gotta do number one *and* number two," he replied with sudden inspiration.

He peered out the window again. He just might be able to make it down. He spun the toilet paper roll a couple of times and ran the faucet.

Basil upended a metal wastebasket and stepped on it, hoisting his right leg over the sill, and then the left, as he clutched the window frame. He eased across the ledge to the metal ladder, and found the rungs. He wished he hadn't taken off his shoes when he came home, but it was too late now.

Warthogs and Feathers

The ladder rattled and creaked. It was obviously not something that had been inspected recently, if at all. He dropped to the ground as he heard the sound of banging on the bathroom door, and darted down the ally toward the back of the building. He could see the shadow of a man near the street. Perhaps a friend of Alto's, assigned to be a look out.

He decided he shouldn't look like he was fleeing a crime scene, even though he realized his house had become one. Basil adjusted his pace to a casual jaunt and smiled. "Good evening," he said pleasantly.

The shadow nodded but after hearing a beep on his cell phone, dashed past Basil down the alley in the direction of loud shouting. Basil quickly resumed his race to the next alley and the next. His socks had torn and he was out of breath when he came upon a pile of empty cartons. *Good enough for hiding for the time being*, he thought, as he covered himself with them.

More shouting and footsteps that became distant. Basil wadded packing paper and stuffed some in his ears before closing his eyes. He needed to sleep. Dreams interrupted his fitful efforts. Something brushing against his face. He dreamt of Oscar Wilde planting a special hairball on his pillow. He dreamt of drinky-poos with Bunny, who looked a lot like Shirley with hair like a yak's. He dreamt of Sangria's chickens roasting in his oven, and of something trying to slither inside his collar. Basil shook the paper out of his ears and opened his eyes. He resisted sitting up or moving in case he was being watched by Mac's gang. He reached his right hand to his neck and grabbled the intruder. He would need to squash it. Then it made a mewing sound. Oscar? Could Oscar have escaped Sangria's clutches? No, Oscar wouldn't leave his kittens when they were just born. Basil moved the very small cat, or large kitten in front of his face. It wasn't Oscar. It was the color of an ice cream sandwich. Basil decided it was a tiny old kitten, and a hungry one based on its dull fur and lack of substance on its frame.

The kitten snuggled. "We are on the run," Basil whispered. "I guess you'll fit in my pocket. We need to find you some food and a place for us to hide until I can make a plan."

Basil had no plan. He didn't know if it was safe to rise from the boxes, or if it was morning yet. He couldn't go home and certainly not to work. He couldn't hail a cab. He had no phone. No credit cards. No identity. Just a little cash that Shirley had loaned him a few days earlier. She was kind about when it needed to be repaid.

That could be a good thing, he realized. He could start over. Reinvent himself. What name? It would not be Herb. Mac would locate him immediately. What name? Dresden. Dresden. Where had he heard that name? A character in Kenly Pope's book? Yes, Dresden might be a good first name. He couldn't remember Dresden's last name, but Smith might work. Not so unusual that it would catch attention. No, he didn't feel like answering to Dresden. Why had his mother named him Basil? It was a terrible name for a child. He would have preferred to be a Fred or a Bob. He needed something simple. Something plain. Harry, perhaps. It was jovial and regal in a friendly way. Yes, he would be Harry. Now for a last name. Something literary or musical. Tilde, Fermata, Credenza. He decided Tilde was easier for the police to spell if he were picked up again. "Harry Tilde," said Basil to the kitten. And now a name for you. He closed his eyes and let his mind wander over names of great writers. "I will call you Truman Capote," he said. "Truman Capote for short, and no nickname." He briefly wondered if Truman was a she, but decided it really didn't matter.

He slid a section of box off his face and realized that it was still dark. Maybe it was always dark in the alley. Then he heard the recycling truck that scooped up cardboard, bottles and plastics on Thursdays. Its hydraulic arm tossed the detritus into the vehicle's crusher. He had about ten minutes to make a plan to find a safer spot.

"Let's go, Truman Capote," whispered Basil. "We need food, and shoes, at least for me."

Basil darted into a doorway, looked around carefully, then flattened himself into the next. He carefully avoided lights until he had to cross a street. There was only an occasional car or bicyclist. On to the next alley and the next until he reached a large park with benches and trash cans that hadn't been emptied yet. Crumpled near the top of one was the remains of a hamburger from a food truck. Basil wiped the catsup off the piece of meat and offered it to Truman Capote who accepted it gratefully and looked at Basil to see if he had more.

Warthogs and Feathers

Basil did not, but vowed to keep looking.

He wished that someone had abandoned a fresh donut and black coffee for him.

What now? His mind wandered to Mrs. Joyce Royce. Would she take him in? Did she really mean for him to call her Bunny? Would Mac be staking out her place as well? Probably. The gang leader knew too much. In his heart Basil knew Mrs. Joyce Royce would help him. He had to try.

Her apartment was on the corner of W. 35th and Celery, a short block named in 1925 by the owner of a vegetable stand. There was an historic marker on the corner that explained the reasoning, even though the green grocer had long been bought out and the store replaced by a Cuban bakery. He had had coffee and pastry there that afternoon with Mrs. Joyce Royce.

It had not been a wise decision on his part, he reflected, when Shirley had noticed bits of donut glaze on his right shoulder. He tried to brush them off as dandruff. Shirley called the dermatologist. But that was years earlier when Mrs. Joyce Royce was still working at O.O.&O. and her long legs and tight skirts quickened his heart and brightened his day.

He would find her, and she would kind and helpful. She would fix him a hearty breakfast and good coffee.

He found 35th, mostly by good luck. Traffic was still light at this early hour. Truman Capote seemed restless in his pocket. Basil found a scrap of cheese next to a trash can and gave it to his new companion. There was Celery Way. His heart raced. Mrs. Joyce Royce's building was in sight. So was a cab idling in front of it. Basil pivoted around Celery Way. Perhaps her building had a back entrance. It did not. Only fire escapes. He wished he could remember what floor she was on or the apartment number from when he had followed her that morning. He looked longingly at every window and sneezed loudly. A window opened. And Mrs. Joyce Royce's face and bare shoulders appeared.

"Bunny," he blurted.

"Shhh," was her response. "Don't try to come up. You must flee. They are looking for you."

"But, Bunny, I have no where to go. And I need breakfast and cat food. Socks and shoes. Sweater. Money. You."

Mrs. Joyce Royce, her hair in large curlers, appeared to be considering his requests. She closed her window and turned out the light. Basil was stunned. Five minutes later the window opened and hands dropped a pillow to the ground near him before it closed again. Basil realized the pillow in a large case had cushioned the sound of things stuffed within it. A pop-lid of a can of tuna. Two $20 bills, $10 worth of subway tokens, socks and a pair of man's shoes, a size larger than Basil wore, and Grinch Christmas socks. A brown golf hat. And a peanut butter sandwich with mayo. Plus a note. "Basil, you must never mention this. And don't come back. JR."

He was shocked. Was this permanent rejection? Basil pressed the fragrant pillow against his face. It was the same coconut and jasmine scent that stirred him at work. He could not abandon it in the alley. At least not all of it. He pulled out a handful of memory foam and placed it in his pocket. After slipping on his new shoes and socks, he fed Truman Capote, ate half his sandwich and headed back out on Celery Way, but not past the front of Mrs. Joyce Royce's building. He knew the cab would still be there. And maybe a lookout or two.

As traffic picked up for the early commute, and there were more pedestrians heading for work, Basil ducked through a park's wrought-iron gate with a squirrel motif and found a bench under a cluster of small trees. He needed time to figure out what he would to do next.

He extracted Truman Capote from his pocket and set him on the bench, then popped off the tuna can's lid. Truman Capote immediately purred and rubbed until Basil placed a quarter of the contents on the slats. The rest would be saved for later. He tucked his old socks in the toes of his new shoes to make them fit better. He dared not carry the pillow with him and after one more moment of hugging it, tossed it in a nearby trash container, but kept the case for his old clothes and food. He wrapped the rest of the tuna's contents in his empty sandwich bag, and told Truman Capote that they had to be going, not sure if the cat would follow. But it did. Then Basil realized he had no idea of where to go, especially in daytime. He found another wooden bench with concrete legs that looked like they were a favorite watering spot for dogs. Basil sat. Truman Capote sniffed the grass and peed.

Basil lost track of time. Only survival and secrecy were important now. It was liberating. He searched for food scraps and shelter in the alleys with his faithful kitten, not far from his new favorite bench. He was increasingly impressed with his resourcefulness. It reminded him of taking survival skills during a week of day camp. He had made a lanyard for his mother, and had roasted marshmallows. He knew camp activities might come in handy some day, but the camp leaders hadn't explained how to deal with this situation. He found missions distributing food and shelter without asking questions. They always had tidbits for the kitten. When he had lots of money again, he would make generous donations to them, he decided.

Emboldened by his success in avoiding detection, he decided it was safe to sit in the large shady park near his former office area and high-end shops and see if anyone left food behind when they returned to work. He knew his former staff never sought fresh air or exercise during their breaks, and Sangria would never want to be seen where their might be bird droppings or children. Mac would only cruise the main streets and alleys. Basil would be safe if he were careful. His homeless look, dirty clothes, and growing stubble were a protective disguise.

"You're in my seat," said a woman with a shopping cart filled with blankets.

"Sorry," replied Basil. "I didn't know it was reserved." He immediately regretted his sarcasm and looked for another bench. Spotting one about ten feet away, he walked over and sat, placing the bulgy pillow case at his feet. Truman Capote followed indirectly.

Then, to his surprise, he saw her. Mora. He hadn't expected to find anyone he knew in the park. Mora had always gone to lunch with Amanda and her friends. How careless of him. She might have noticed him through an office window and decided to look for him in the park. He pulled his hat down and his collar up to hide his long neck. She sat on the other end of the bench and opened her yak purse, removed a container filled with sprouts and little yellow things. When she glanced in his direction, Basil rummaged through his pillow case. He wondered if he coughed, like he had something contagious, perhaps she would leave. He coughed several times. But instead of leaving, she handed him an antique hanky with tiny letters stitched on it from her purse. One that looked vaguely familiar. Was it another gift that he had forgotten or was it Amanda's?

He accepted the hanky and coughed into it. Unfortunately she didn't seem remotely alarmed by his visage or possible illness. Instead, she asked, "What's your name, sir?"

What was his new name? Fred? Marvin? No, it was Harry. Harry something. "Harry Bunch," he said, coughing dryly again and leaving the hanky over his mouth.

"Are you well?" she asked.

He nodded. "Allergies," he said, muffling his voice with the cloth.

She rummaged in her yak purse and pulled out a small bottle with a greenish liquid. He remembered that it was a pea juice. She had a sip and looked at him as if she had many questions.

"Harry, have you had anything to eat? I have plenty to share," Mora said with genuine concern. "I lived hand-to-mouth years ago to see what it was like. Part of a project on street people." She waited, hoping he would share more about himself.

Basil was hungry enough to consider trying the sprouts that she offered, but instead told her that he was fine.

"When I was working on a project after returning from Nepal to Goa, I learned that people who didn't have a home, had a certain lost look about them. If I may ask, and this isn't intended to sound rude, how long have you been, uh, in this situation?" asked Mora.

"A while," said Basil. "I can't remember."

"You remind me of someone," she said after a few minutes. "Actually of my father. But a lot of older men start to resemble each other. It's sort of like new babies look like Winston Churchill."

Basil did not respond and lowered his head.

"We're quite worried about him. He's missing," Mora added.

Basil cleared his throat and mumbled, "What happened?"

Mora gazed out across the park. A tall elderly man walking a St. Bernard had caught her eye.

"All right, I'll tell you because maybe you will see him somewhere and will give him this message for us. Tell him, 'All is forgiven. Come home.'"

Basil coughed and raised the hanky to cover his nose as well as mouth.

"Okay, Harry, here's the story. It is so crazy that I can't believe it. He's wanted for bank- and grave-robbery, but I don't think that is true at all. He just got caught up in a mess and he's on the run. Not like him at all. He is a sweet, quiet academic sort and near retirement, but easily manipulated especially by bullies. Doesn't know how to deal with them. Do you know what I mean? And people say he collects warthogs. Strange but interesting."

Basil nodded and studied his hands, covering his ring finger.

"I came halfway around the world to get to know him after all these years, then this happened. I have very little childhood memory of him. Mother was one of those difficult people. And so jealous. She thought he was having an affair with someone who actually liked his etudes or sharps or whatever they were. But here I am, going on and on and I have to get back to work tending chickens and now six kittens at a publishing house. Can you believe that? Well, hope to see you again, Harry. Remember, If you spot my dad, tell him we'll help him in court. We'll bail him out. We have witnesses, including a cab driver, to prove his innocence or what there is of it."

With that, Mora said maybe she'd see him again tomorrow, and headed in the direction of the office, leaving the hanky with him.

Basil wondered as he watched her walk across the park, what does "all is forgiven" mean? Obviously not the crimes of which he was accused. Could Shirley be ready for a reconciliation now that she knew he was a criminal not a philanderer?

He had no idea, but he was touched by Mora's concern but alarmed that they might call in a cab driver as a potential witness.

Truman Capote had returned and rubbed against his leg. It was time to move on. Basil didn't know where to go. In a moment of inspiration, he decided to follow the cat. That plan lasted about fifteen minutes, but made Basil smile for the first time in days. Truman Capote led him through students lounging on blankets, past three children flying kites, a duck pond, where he and the cat stopped to watch frogs. The cat stalked a frog on the edge of the water, while Basil looked on from a less muddy distance. Basil realized that during all his years working at O.O.&O. he had never taken a walk through the park during his lunch hour. He should have, instead of eating at his desk, or worse yet sitting through another "working lunch" with Sangria. Then, as Truman Capote, tail twitching, crept up on a squirrel, Basil noticed the police. A pair entered the park and stopped to talk with people on benches. They were showing them a piece of paper, and after heads shook no, they went on to the next bench or cluster of people. Then they were headed in his direction. Truman Capote chased the squirrel up an oak tree. Basil wished he could follow. He dropped the pillow case behind a trash basket hoping it wouldn't be noticed.

"Excuse me, sir," said the first officer. "Sorry to bother you, but we are trying to locate this gentleman."

Basil lowered his hat's brim even farther, and peered at the paper. The picture taken by Amanda was of Basil on his twenty-fifth anniversary with Shirley. He was well-shaven, was without his trifocals, and wearing a tux. Beaming, in fact. They were going out to the Village Lighthouse for a sumptuous crab cake dinner, an evening that was only marred by food poisoning. He was touched that Shirley had provided that picture from years ago, to the police.

"Who's he?" Basil said in his new affected voice.

"Basil Beale. We can't say much because it's an ongoing investigation," said the officer, "but if you see him, approach carefully. He may look harmless, but, we think he's part of a most unusual criminal gang."

Basil nodded. He had escaped detection so far, but he didn't know if Mrs. Joyce Royce would continue to protect him or turn him in, describing the clothes she had given him for his getaway. Or would Mora, as she began to think more about the man on the bench who reminded her of her father? She seemed genuinely concerned. He would look for her at lunchtime tomorrow. But, he wondered, how could all be forgiven if the police were still looking for him?

13

And she was there again, on the bench, looking around the park. When Mora saw him she waved and patted on the bench as if she had saved a seat. Basil ambled over, trying not too appear to eager, and sat down again at the opposite end. He was edgy, fearful that she would recognize him and turn him in, but she was family, and caring, he hoped.

"I'm so glad you came," she said. "I've brought a sandwich for you and something for your cat." She popped open a can of tuna. Truman Capote was at her feet immediately.

"What did you say his name is?"

Basil cleared his throat. "He's not my cat. I call him Truman Capote."

"A stray," she said thoughtfully. "I've wanted a cat since I moved into my own apartment a week ago. It's an unusual name. My father had a cat named Oscar Wilde, who turned out to be female and has kittens. We're raising them in our office."

Basil was about to ask how the kittens were doing, but thought better of it. Mora reached over with his sandwich wrapped in paper rather than plastic. She looked at his fingers. "You have long fingers? Did you ever play the piano?"

Basil bit hungrily into his food without answering. Truman Capote circled Mora's legs, rubbing and purring.

"I've had a great idea," said Mora. "You look like you need a job and a place to stay. There is something very trustworthy about you or I wouldn't make the offer, and we could do this without letting my family know. Don't say no. You could sleep on the couch, and I know I could get a job for you at the place I work. But you'd need a haircut and a shave. They recently advertised an opening in the mail room—sorting the manuscripts as they come in and sending them to the right departments. We're also getting a lot of fan mail for Kenly Pope in anticipation of the latest book. It's being fast-tracked. Pope is just a pen name, but clout at the publishing house. And guess what? The galleys will be off press tonight. But that's a huge secret. Don't tell."

That wasn't a surprise to Basil. He always felt there was something strange about the push for the book to be printed despite its quality. But then there was Mora's lovely offer to stay with her.

"I couldn't possibly," said Basil. "Thanks. And your secret is safe with me."

Mora was quiet for a moment then said, "I was afraid you would turn me down for housing. But just think about it. You don't have to decide today. You seem like a nice man and I'd just like to help you get back on your feet."

She passed him two oatmeal raisin cookies. "Healthy," she noted. "It's modified from a family recipe."

My recipe. I used to make them for you, thought Basil. He glanced at Truman Capote. The cat had jumped into Mora's lap. His eyes were closed and he was purring even louder.

Mora petted the cat and tried to stroke out some of the tangles of black and white fur.

"Do you mind, Harry, if he comes home with me since he's just a stray?"

Basil turned his face away. He would miss Truman Capote's company, but he wouldn't have to worry about feeding him or caring for him. He knew that cats need lots of attention. Look at Oscar Wilde. Hairballs, then pregnancy. Constant vet bills. Besides, Truman Capote wasn't his. Sometimes cats only pretend they are your cat until something better comes along. He knew Truman Capote was like that. And Mora would take better care of him than most people would. He hoped that the cat wouldn't end up in Sangria's clutches. But there was little he could do about that or anything anymore.

"Okay," he said, reaching to touch Truman Capote's head one last time. The cat pulled away. "He's yours."

"See you tomorrow," Mora said, tucking Truman Capote in her large bag. "I'll let you know how he's doing. Full report and pictures on my phone."

Basil watched her walk back across the park and contemplated her offer. How nice it would be to sleep on a bed. To have someone to talk with. A job again, no matter how menial. It was all so tempting but dangerous to his future. He had only been on the lam for a few weeks. So far, except for the fearful time while escaping Mac and his gang, it hadn't been so bad, No, he would keep up the illusion—meet with her one more time on the park bench—and have a plan by then for his future. But he couldn't think of one. He had no day to seize anymore.

And there she was the next day, fifteen minutes late according to the large Victorian-looking clock in the center of the park near a fountain of a large peeing dog, perhaps inspired by the park's architect. It always attracted crowds of small boys and mothers who dragged them away. Basil had always thought the statue was tasteless, like the one erected in tribute to the Ozburns. But many statues were like that, or at least the water needed to be redirected and a blanket tossed over the dog's leg. That's what he would tell a camera crew if they were doing a man-in-the-street interview with him about the dog and whether or not it was appropriate for a public place, even though real dogs were doing it on every tree.

Mora apologized when she took her seat at the other end of the bench. "My boss, Sangria, had some last-minute chores for me. Chores," she repeated. She pulled out two cheese and sprout wraps from her bag. "Don't worry, it's real cheese. My sister Amanda always wants me to be a vegan, but sometimes I prefer the real stuff."

Basil mumbled a thanks.

"Looks like rain," said Mora.

Basil nodded in agreement.

"Have you thought any more about my offer? You know the one to stay with me?"

Basil said, "Sorry. I can't. Other plans."

Mora looked at him in disbelief. "I don't mean to pry, but I doubt that very much. I think you are running from something and you need a safe place to hangout where you'll be comfortable and have good meals. I'm a creative cook."

"I'm leaving on a short trip," he said. "I'll be gone a while."

Mora looked concerned. "Doing what? Where?"

"It's rather private," said Basil. "I'm not allowed to say." There, he had come up with something, even if the plan was totally undeveloped.

"Harry, wait, I just had a great idea. I can help you get away. You need to take a vacation. I just need a couple of days to put my idea together and assemble what you will need to travel." Mora studied his face and added, "I've traveled the world and know what travelers need for a journey. Best yet, I can help you find a place to go. Winter's coming and you don't want to sleep in the alleys if you won't accept my offer of a place to stay."

Basil nodded appreciatively.

"Great," she said.

She pulled out her cell phone and showed him pictures of Truman Capote lounging on a chair that looked like one that Shirley had given Mora for the apartment. He wanted to ask about Shirley, but he didn't dare. He wanted to ask about Oscar and the kittens. He wanted to know if Mac was in jail or still out looking for him. He just wanted to sleep in his comfortable bed.

She looked at her watch. "Gotta run. A meeting about Kenly Pope's launch. See you in three days."

Three days seemed like a long time. Basil was both afraid she wouldn't show up, and that she would. What could she be planning? Basil made sure he arrived eight minutes early according to the large clock at the west corner of the park, to take his usual seat before anyone else claimed it. He wished he had a wet cloth to wipe off all the pigeon droppings, both new and historic, on the dark brown slats. The occasional heavy rain had not been cleansing.

Basil felt an autumn chill in the breeze and looked for Mora. He wished he had asked Mrs. Joyce Royce to toss down a heavy jacket and blanket or two. But instead of spotting Mora, he saw a bag lady heading in his direction. He knew that was politically incorrect to think ill of her, with her faded pink shawl pulled over her hand, long flowered dress and red sneakers, in those terms. After all, he was a street person himself, but the woman was carrying a stuffed plastic bag draped over her shoulder. He hoped she would not see the open seats on his bench, but she did. Not far behind her was Mora. She seemed to be hurrying to overtake the woman and get to the bench first. But that was not to be. The bag lady sat next to Basil in the middle of the bench after she dropped the bag at her feet. She seemed to be breathing hard from the exertion.

When Mora arrived, she gave the woman a glance that Basil could not interpret. Mora sat down at the far end of the bench and said nothing. Basil could hear her rummaging in her purse, probably for his lunch, and he was hungry enough to want tofu.

She passed the food to the woman who handed it to Basil. He wondered if he should share with the stranger, but decided not.

Once she caught her breath, without a word, the woman stood up and left.

"Wait, you left your bag," he called.

"Let her go," said Mora. "I told you I would bring things you need for travel. I couldn't very well take them to the office you know, with all the security these days so I paid her to help."

Basil was astonished. "You have gone to so much trouble for me. I don't understand."

She studied his face and said, "As soon as you finish your lunch, take this bag into the porta-potty over there and change and pack. It's all there, including your ticket. Read the note, then get to the station and be on your way. And by the way, there's one more surprise in the bag. Wrapped in brown paper. Something to read on the bus."

Basil was stunned. He opened the plastic bag to peek inside, and saw a wallet, passport and sandals, new clothes and a small duffle bag. Before he could say thanks, Mora was on her feet and heading back to the office.

He called out to her, "Wait." Mora turned back and smiled. "Carpe diem," she said.

Carpe diem. She must know who I am. How did she know? Why is she helping? Can I trust her? What options do I have as fall is turning to winter.? She had been so kind. She said she had always wanted to find me. Of course she'd wants to help me.

He had no choice but to follow her directions. Basil went directly to the porta-potty, the handicapped one because it had more space. He changed into the docker shorts and floral printed shirt—nothing he ever would have purchased. After stuffing his old clothes in a nearby trash can, he put on his new floppy hat and sat on a different bench to look at the contents of a brown envelope and his new wallet and watch.

No credit cards but lots of cash in various denominations. A new passport in the name of Harry Bunch. A clever forgery with a Photoshopped picture of himself. He looked younger with more hair and granny glasses.

He found the one-way ticket. A bus leaving at six for Miami, then for a second bus to Key West.

Key West. A place Shirley had wanted to visit, but he had never had the time, even when they had been in Miami for that book fair.

Key West. A lot of people were starting new lives there and in Florida and nobody seemed to care what their former lives had been like or what they were running from. Basil looked at his watch and realized he needed to be at the bus station soon. He hoped the station would have a café or a food truck. He longed for a greasy burger and fries. A new life as a unapologetic carnivore.

14

The seats were filled for the first hours of the three-day trip, but after the first stops, including one at an Interstate truck area, Basil was glad to see the number of passengers decreased. And he was quite relieved that before midnight, the large man, who smelled like an ashtray after every break, departed into the night.

Basil was unable to sleep as he relived the events of the past few weeks, stranger than some of the works of fiction that he had read and rejected. As much as he missed what he had considered the normal life of having a family, a cat, a job, albeit increasingly stressful lately, it had overall been, well, relatively normal. After all those years at Ozburn, Ozburn & Ozburn, he had expected a laudatory farewell—perhaps not the fancy retirement party that Shirley expected, but at least a cake in the office, and tributes from his colleagues. He suspected, however, the interns would not have anything good to say, and certainly not Darwin or Sangria, unless they felt obliged. They had forced him to be someone other than himself, the dedicated, steadfast, reliable, elder statesman, dean of the dictionary and style manuals. He knew where commas went, the difference between effect and affect. And he had an eye for good books, not the trash that increasingly appeared on his desk. He realized that he was glad to be rid of responsibility for Kenly Pope's tomes. They might indeed be best sellers because of the publisher's investment in promotions, but he didn't have to put his stamp on approval on this author's book.

His thoughts drifted to Mrs. Joyce Royce and wondered what would happened to the warthog collection. He hoped that Darwin had sold

He awoke to his seatmate on her feet, crouching over him as she tried to straddle his legs to get to the aisle. The bus was lurching on a stretch of unpaved highway through a construction zone. Harry moved as quickly as he could to avoid her long hair brushing his face as she attempted to climb over him.

"Watch my stuff," she said. She bumped into seats as she staggered to the toilet at the back. Basil realized this might be the moment to seize. He grabbed his duffle and found an empty seat about three rows back on the left side. He settled by the window and placed his duffle in the seat by the aisle.

Then began the pounding and shouting of "Help me! Let me out!"

Several passengers hurried toward the back, then called to Chad, the driver, to pull over. He edged between no stopping signs in the work zone, and set his blinkers. Then with a face of annoyance rather than concern, pushed his way through the rescuers to the rear. Chad couldn't open the door either. Basil, who by now was kneeling on his seat to have a view without getting involved, watched as several fellow passengers focused their cellphones on the driver and the toilet door. The driver, a short man, who looked like he should have stopped for a nap, a few hours earlier, tried to calm down Rita, but she wouldn't stop screaming and her vocabulary included words that would be bleeped on later newscasts after passengers' videos were aired on social media.

The door wouldn't budge. Chad finally threw up his hands and yelled, "Sorry, but you are going to have to stay there until we can get to a mechanic." More screaming and pounding ensued as he made his way back to the front of the bus. Chad paused when he neared Basil. "Your daughter will have to stay there for a while. Sorry."

Basil replied, "But, sir, she's not my daughter."

"She said you would say that when she changed her seat to be with you."

As the driver stormed back to his seat, a woman tapped Basil on the shoulder, "Mister," she said. "Your daughter is crying out for you. Have you no heart? You should at least go back and calm her."

Basil said emphatically, "As I told the driver, she's not my daughter, no matter what she says. Never saw her before this trip."

The woman eyed him harshly. "She says your name is Harry and the two of you are going to Key West to make up for lost time in your lives. She's your poor long-lost daughter. And she knows a lot about what's in your duffle. Now how do you explain that, Harry?"

Basil sighed, placed his duffle in the overhead bin above his original seat, and walked slowly to the back as the bus eased forward into traffic. He tried not to return the hostile gazes of fellow travelers. As he reached the toilet door he could hear the heaving sobs of Rita, wailing that she had been abandoned once again by Daddy. He resisted the urge to kick the door and stuff her head in the toilet bowl and push the vacuum flush. Instead he said, "Rita, did you try sliding the latch? Move it from the word that says CLOSED, to one that say OPEN."

The sobbing subsided. He heard the sound of the latch sliding. The door opened and she squeezed out attempting to fall into his arms.

"Daddy saved me!" she shouted. He stumbled backwards to avoid her hug, and was embarrassed by the loud clapping for her rescue, except for the woman who had spoken harshly a few moments earlier. "Humph," she said. "Some father you are to not help her immediately."

Basil waited for Rita to take her seat by the window, and he squeezed back into his seat next to her.

"How did I do?" she asked

"Do what?" asked Basil with disgust. "That was quite a performance."

"That's what I hoped," she said. "I'd like a career in theater so I have to perfect my skills whenever I can."

She looked out the window, rolling a long strand of bleached hair around her fingers.

"At the next stop I'll buy you lunch," she said.

"I thought you don't have any money," said Basil.

"I don't. But you do, and I'll pay you back when we get to Key West. You have enough to support both of us there."

"I'm not going to support you and that's final," said Basil.

"We'll see," she said. She smiled and closed her eyes.

After her breathing suggested that she was sleeping, Basil retrieved the wrapped package from his duffle. He wondered why the package was described by Mora as a surprise. He carefully peeled off the tape that Rita had resealed badly and opened the brown paper. Inside was a bound galley that publishers printed on cheap paper to hand out to reviewers and people in the trade to give them a sneak preview of a new book. There was always a disclaimer on the cover to let readers know that it was an uncorrected page proof, meaning that even if it was carefully edited, if a small mistake was found, the book wasn't in its final form before printing. There would be blurbs of praise, and information about the author, the publication date, estimated size of the press and that sort of information.

His first glimpse showed that this galley was bound in hot pink paper with dark purple ink. His second glimpse provoked a noticeable gasp: *The Devine Royalty Social Club Queen's Son. Author: Kenly Pope.* He turned it over. There was predictable praise with blurbs solicited from other noted authors, who probably had never seen even a chapter. And a photograph of the mysterious Kenly Pope. Basil studied it closely. The shadowed face was in profile, a large hat tipped to the camera blocking specific features that would identify the author.

The cutline added to the mystery. "Kenly Pope, raised with a keen understanding of literature and publishing, makes the author debut under a pseudonym. The mask will come off when the book tour begins."

So, the name is definitely a fake. Is it just to get publicity? That would cause a stir no matter how trite and poorly written the book is. But why should Mora find this interesting to me? I walked away from that book and my job. I really don't care if it is a best seller or not. If this was Mora's idea of a present, well, I have no plans to ever read it again. He slipped it back in the brown wrapper and stowed it once again in the overhead bin.

Rita still seemed to be asleep, but he couldn't be sure of that either. He tried to get his long legs in a comfortable position without stretching into the aisle. Mora should have purchased Amtrak tickets instead of the budget bus. He shouldn't be judgemental. She was the only one in the family trying to help him escape arrest and probably life in prison. He had edited enough crime stories to know that he had no alibi. Was "helpless" an alibi? Was "carpe diem" ever an alibi?"

He looked beyond Rita's splayed form to see what the scenery, if the landscape on I-95 could be described as such, revealed. The hardwoods were now mixed with more pines and a few palms. LAST GAS BEFORE FLORIDA JUST 99 MILES AND 99 SMILES.

Florida. That long thin peninsula. Miami was still hundreds of miles away, and Key West way beyond that. Free cup of orange juice at welcome station. Then on a faded billboard: Visit Gator Village: AN OVER 60 GATED COMMUNITY WITH REAL GATORS IN EVERY POND.

The bus pulled into the visitor's center at the state line, and passengers were told to limit their break to fifteen minutes. Basil was glad to stretch his legs, and find the men's room. No fast food, but there were short lines at the vending machines for candy bars, crackers, and another for soft drinks. *Not exactly a healthy substitute for lunch*, Basil thought.

A woman was cursing the candy machine and kicking it. "Took my money and didn't give me a damn thing. Piece of junk!" She left.

The Milky Way bar slowly dropped, and was retrieved by a teenager who quickly pocketed it and drifted back to the bus.

The driver was honking. Basil sighed and strode back without making a purchase.

"What dja get for me?" asked Rita. Basil could see that she had been into his bag again. It was turned around.

"Damn it," he muttered.

Rita gave him a look. "I needed something to read," she said, "and you didn't seem interested in this book."

He recognized the pink cover. At first he welled with anger, then realized he really didn't care. His only plan for the book was to dump it when he arrived in Key West. Maybe in a laundromat. People were always looking for something to read in places like that.

"Suit yourself."

"I just started it," she said. "I read everything. Did you see the dedication page?"

He shook his head as he tried to arrange himself in his seat.

"I'm not sure what this means but it is dedicated to B.R.B. Jr. always my inspiration," she read. "How touching."

Basil said, "Let me see that." His brows furrowed. Those are my initials. It must be a coincidence. I don't know Kenly Pope. The scribbled handwriting was large and deliberate. An affected flair that new authors often employ using a thick pen point. The ink was purple.

Rita continued, "When my book comes out, I will have to carefully consider my dedication. Sometimes it is more interesting than the plot. Did you know I was planning to write a book, Harry? That's why I'm going to Key West, to become a crime writer. There's got to be a lot of fugitives there, living under assumed names and getting jobs on fishing boats where they can become drug smugglers and hide their loot in the Bahamas or Caymans. You know that kind of book. Maybe you can help me, Harry. I bet you have connections because you are so mysterious and have cash, no credit cards, no driver's license and just a pink book in your bag."

Basil was barely listening to her prattle. He was trying to think why his initials were attached to a book that he disliked so intensely, one he had tried to scuttle in his last days with the Ozzies. None of the interns would have inscribed that even if they were capable of diagramming a sentence. Darwin. Not even Darwin. He would have dedicated the book to himself.

Rita nudged him sharply. "I was talking to you, Harry, and you weren't listening at all."

"Sorry," said Basil. "I was thinking about the dedication. You're right, it is quite astonishing. Please tell me what you think about the story."

Rita beamed. "I was hoping you'd say that. I always got Bs on my book reports. I got knocked down for spelling. Lots of red ink from old Mr. Marzipan. That's what we called him. Did you ever teach, Harry? Would you have assigned this book to your class? Of course it has naughty bits, like when Ashley and Dresden go off in the . . ."

She realized that Harry had leaned back, eyes closed.

"Oh wait, you asked what I thought. Best-seller for sure. A movie or television series. Everyone will want to dress like Ashley. She has that look, described so well. A big hit. I've never been wrong about a book." Rita nudged Basil and smiled smugly.

Basil grunted. "Perhaps you're right. It's not my genre." He knew immediately he shouldn't have given her an opener for further conversation. He should have left it at a grunt, or a "mmm."

"I like all kinds of genre, Harry," she continued. "Romance, adventure, mystery, YA, if they have some adult moments, like Judy Blume's books. First time I knew that people talked in a book about getting their periods. Yikes! Not in our house. We didn't talk. Did you?"

"No, I never did."

"Well, we heard our mother talking about hers and it was pretty gross."

Basil was alarmed about where this revelation would lead. "So what's your favorite book?" he asked.

"This one. It's always the one I'm reading because I can remember it the best. I read really fast and I have a photographic memory that self-deletes after I finish a page. Did you ever hear of that ability before, Harry? I think it's a medical mystery."

"Very unusual," he said, trying to figure out how soon they might reach Miami. A road sign had not been promising. He wasn't sure where they were. It was still early and they wouldn't change buses in Miami until evening.

"Do you have more books with you, Harry? Or do I have to read this one again?"

"Read it again. I'm going to take a nap." He knew he couldn't sleep but pretending would perhaps stop her rambling and he could think about his new life. He wanted to focus on that but he couldn't get the events of recent weeks out of his head. Things were fine, he had thought, until the month before retirement. He had remained a quiet, no-nonsense boss, one of the last of his generation, asking no favors, ignoring the not-so-subtle antics of his young staff. The interns. He had tried to follow the directives of Sangria, flighty, vindictive and feather-brained. He had righted his warthogs and uncoupled them daily.

He could no longer remember how he had gotten involved with Mac or why he agreed to go to the zoo or why Shirley had left him. He had not done anything wrong, even if circumstantially it didn't look good. Or why Mora, a daughter he barely knew, was helping him flee and establish a new identity in Key West. Why? She had mentioned that all was forgiven and he should turn himself in. Not likely. He knew how long Shirley could hold a grudge. She didn't speak to her second cousin, Peewee, for fifteen years, after Peewee won a baking contest in which Shirley had expected to garner the gold medal. She suspected that Betty Crocker had given Peewee the edge with her double chocolate (box) cake. Shirley ignored the presentation aspect of the judging. It was hard to escape that just as she finished frosting her lemony white cake (made from scratch) that her dog had bitten off four inches of one side. She had applied extra frosting on that area, but the heat in her car on the way to the fair grounds, had caused a bit of frosting avalanche. Shirley, to this day, believed that the judges should have focused only on the entries' flavors. Her relationship with Peewee is now cordial but strained. Shirley would likely be more vengeful now, believing that he was having an affair with Mrs. Joyce Royce. Ah, Bunny. Were those Mr. Joyce Royce's clothes in her apartment? Or was there someone else in her life? Basil would rather think that Mr. Joyce Royce had left the clothes behind when he left, at her mandate, because she wanted a divorce.

Basil felt a nudge from his seatmate, and pretended to snore as he turned his head toward the aisle. Perhaps a Snickers bar at the next stop would help. He'd get one for her too. Anything to shut her up.

He slept fitfully most of the day until they reached the bus station in Miami much later than scheduled. There had been long delays in construction zones in Georgia and three major accidents in Florida.

Rita tugged at his arm and said it was time to get off.

"Let's hire a car to drive us the rest of the way, Harry. It will be so much faster. And we can split the tab."

"No. No. I have a ticket. I'm not going to pay for a cab, car, trolley or limo," said Basil, as he grabbed his duffle and checked to be sure his book was inside. It wasn't.

"Where's my book," he said angrily.

"I'm sitting on it. Try and get it and I'll scream," said Rita.

Basil turned and left the bus. He checked to be sure he still had his wallet, papers and ticket for the transfer bus to Key West. It was a small sea-blue vehicle painted with murals of shells, divers, pirates and famous performers on Mallory Square in Key West. The Cat Man and the new Cookie Lady, fire swallower and trained potbelly racing pigs. The new driver had a shoulder-length blond curls and wore a captain's hat. He handed each passenger a tourist brochure to read along the way. Basil was relieved to see there were single seats on each side of the aisle and chose the one nearest the driver, who introduced himself as Marlin Bates.

The seat across from Basil was quickly taken by an elderly woman with a cane. She was dressed in a flowing white gown and wore aviator sunglasses, even though it was almost dark. Her wispy grayish hair seemed to be styled too long for her age. She could sit on it.

When the bus was almost full, Rita barreled up the steps shouting, "Harry? Harry? Where's my daddy? Harry."

Basil didn't answer, but it was difficult to pretend not to hear her when she was almost in front of him.

"Oh, there you are. You forgot your book. Harry, dear. I hope you're not disappointed but I've decided to stay in Miami for a few days, then take a car. I'll see you in Key West."

She tossed the book to him and blew a kiss. Basil watched her head toward a red Mercedes. A silver-haired man in a Hawaiian print shirt bowed and opened the passenger's door for her. *How does she do it so quickly?* Basil wondered. *But good riddance.*

Marlin closed the door, tapped his microphone and announced that although it was early in the drive for his narrative, he would be providing the history of famous mile markers along the way, including the story of the railroad, hurricane and bridges, and tell everyone about the best things to do once they were in the famed destination. And at the first rest stop, once they got out of the city, they could buy conch fritter pancakes. "Just joking," Marlin added, after listening to passenger groans. He apologized for the late start adding that it was likely to be too dark to see much, but he'd give his talk anyway.

Basil was about to tuck the book back in his duffle. It was no longer in pristine condition. Pages were dog-eared, and a large heel print was on the pink cover. He felt a nudge from across the aisle.

"I'd like to read that, Harry, if you're done," said the woman, poking him again with her cane. "I read fast."

Basil shrugged and handed her the book.

She removed a flashlight from her quilted bag and studied the cover. "Love the title. Catchy." She read the dedication out loud. "Lovely." And then she started on chapter one. Out loud.

"What'cha snitchin, Ashly Belor?" The woman looked surprised, but not as much as he might expect. "Nun yer business," said Ash.

"Great beginning," said Basil's fellow passenger. Basil wished that the Marlin would begin his narration, but he was cursing other drivers who taking their time by adhering to the speed limit.

The woman's dramatic reading became louder and when she paused to have a sip of bottled water, the man behind him said, "Keep going, please."

15

Marlin turned on his microphone and again tried to explain the history of the seven-mile bridge they would cross later and how a dramatic scene from the Schwarzenegger film *True Lies* had been filmed there, but the passengers were more interested in listening to the next chapter of the book, the part about when Dresden went back to the club house and was frightened by the lurking stranger. Because they were engaged in the story, they didn't mind unexpected delays involving their bus's flat tire, or when it ran out of gas and it took another hour for fuel to arrive. Instead of a two or three-hour trip, arriving at midnight they would end up in Key West in time for breakfast.

"Where can we get copies?" the man behind him asked.

"No idea," said Basil. He figured they would be getting to Key West in an hour or so, if they didn't get stuck again in traffic on the two-lane highway. He reached in his duffle to read Mora's instructions for when he arrived.

"Dear Dad: Don't take a taxi at the bus stop. Beware of taxis. Buy a ticket for the Conch Train and try to blend in with the tourists. Go to the first stop on Duval Street. Take your first left, and half way down the block you'll see a yellow cottage on the right. It will say NO VACANCY, but you have a reservation in room 4 under your pseudonym. There will be more information at the desk for you. They feed a lot of cats so you will be happy."

Basil became fearful. Why the secrecy? No taxis?

After they crossed to the Stock Island and neared Key West, Basil interrupted the reader and took his copy back.

The woman glared and fellow passengers groaned.

"It will be out soon," said Basil, as he waited for the door to open. A few taxis idled across the street. He avoided them and tried to be inconspicuous as he located a Conch Train stop and bought a ticket. The train wasn't what he expected. It was a bunch of little connected yellow cars with green awnings and open sides pulled by a black locomotive with a smokestack. He felt very exposed sitting on a bench seat where he was visible, especially the profile of his long neck. He nervously gazed at early-morning tourists. He was the only person on the train and the driver, chatting with other "engineers" told him it would be another fifteen minutes before they left. Basil sighed. "Go buy some souvenirs," suggested the engineer. "My uncle Conkie owns the shop. It's open all night."

Basil saw Conkie's Souvenirs across the street. T-shirts, many with naughty messages, filled the windows. He spotted a rack of cheap sunglasses and large straw hats and decided to buy one of each to hopefully add to his disguise. It would replace the one Rita had sat on after she had taken it from his duffle.

Seeing neither clerk and only one customer who had been on both of his buses, Basil punched the bell at the counter. A sunburned squat man, wild floral print shirt, shell-beaded necklace, and with a Cuban cigar crunched between his teeth, emerged from the back of the store. Basil wasn't sure if this was Uncle Conkie, so he said nothing. Neither did the man. But Basil was concerned that the man stared hard at him, glanced at the other customer, and wrote something down after he made change.

Basil walked slowly, like he wasn't on the lam, tore the tags off his sunglasses and hat, and got back on his train seat. He was still the only passenger, and the engineer was no place to be seen.

A woman with an iguana in her bike basket rode by, then returned and said to Basil, "Didn't you see the NO SERVICE sign on the engine? This train is out of commission for the day."

Basil said, "But I have a ticket."

"Oh, well," she said. "He left ten minutes ago, and obviously left you."

"How do I get to the Duval stop?" he asked trying not to sound as frustrated as he felt.

"Walk that way," she pointed. "And watch your step. They haven't cleaned the streets in front of the bars yet. Some are open all night so the party can continue outside."

Basil wondered what Mora was thinking when she booked him to Key West. She hadn't mentioned recommendations or warnings about eateries to avoid. Key Lime pie seemed to be the dessert du jour. Shirley had tried to make it once. Just once. It didn't resemble the glossy picture in the travel magazine, and Basil wondered why it was flavored like mince. She had mumbled something about suggested flavor substitutes.

Basil realized that he was not alone on the street. He turned to see a cab less than half a block behind him. It pulled up next to him and the driver said, "Need a ride, mister? Two bucks anywhere downtown." Not to show his face, Basil mumbled no thanks and waved away the driver. "I'll be back to see if you change your mind," said the cabbie. Basil picked up his pace. He wondered if he should duck behind a store Dumpster until he could reenter the street when there were more pedestrians.

He considered the idea, looked around, and entered a driveway behind a restaurant with a large patio in front for outside dining. Kitchen staff prepping for breakfast were listening to Cuban music. He found a wooden crab trap next to the Dumpster, and sat. Basil open his duffle and searched for Mora's instructions. Had he missed something? No, she had clearly told him to go to the guest house and check in. He was no longer sure that was a good idea. She had made so many arrangements a short time. The daughter he didn't really know and who immediately was hired by Sangria? Immediately bonding with Amanda?

He was becoming paranoid. No, it was all too arranged. And there was conspiracy to tie him to crimes he didn't not commit, but had no alibi for. He would not go to the guest house. Someone would look for him there. He'd find a job and get another alias.

The back door of the restaurant opened and a stocky man in a blood-and gravy-stained apron burst out, apparently not caring where his sandaled feet took him through the scattered trash near the Dumpster. He tossed the bag into the bin, wiped his face and surveyed Basil.

"You don't need to pick the garbage. We got scraps for people like you. You look fancier than most pickers, but some dress up for the streets."

Basil said, "I'm not looking for a handout, but I'd like to buy a cheap breakfast."

"You talk pretty good. Are you looking for work? Rod just quit."

Basil thought for a minute. "Sure. Doing what?"

"Dishes. Rod washed dishes."

Basil thought again. He had no experience in the kitchen. Even after Margo left with Mora, he hadn't washed dishes. He bought TV dinners, and used plastic forks and paper cups. Shirley and Amanda used the dishwasher, but this job was a good temporary opportunity and he didn't need to display proficiency.

"Sure," he said. "When do I start?"

"Now," the man grunted. "Follow me and put your stuff there." He pointed to a shelf in a corner. "I'm Cheek—and you?

"Harry," said Basil, accepting a stained apron and a Broncos cap that wasn't much cleaner. "Rod's," explained Cheek. He led Basil to the back of a small kitchen with its greasy fans going.

A large metal sink and counter faced the large alley window and parking lot. Stacks of sticky breakfast dishes were next to it.

Basil was tempted to snatch a leftover biscuit, but Cheek was watching and soon gave a list of instructions about soap, hot water, scrubbing and drying. "Gotta be fast and efficient. These bad boys gotta be done in thirty minutes for the early lunch crowd. Oh, I promised you something to eat. Here's some bacon and key lime toast. We'll take that out of your first hour's pay."

The food looked like it had been rejected by a customer. But it was edible. Basil scraped the plates, which were embellished with a rooster design, and scrubbed them in the hot water.

"Faster," said Cheek.

The cooks, back from their cigar-smoking break in the parking area, began prepping the mostly chicken and seafood menu for lunch. They shouted in Spanish above the clatter, at times directing comments toward Basil who understood nothing.

"Poco loco," said one, nodding at him.

When he had finished all but three large pots, Cheek told him to take a five-minute break.

Basil cleaned up after the lunch crowd. His hands were raw and his feet and back hurt, but he was proud he had accomplished something, other than just running away from his former life, and Cheek seemed somewhat pleased with his efforts. He even offered him a full course dinner—coleslaw, fried chicken, fried potatoes and key lime pie for supper, with extra coleslaw, when the supper crowd had emptied out. Cheek sat with him.

"You surprise me, Harry. You don't look like the type to tramp around. Are you running? Doesn't matter to me or the owners. We all running from something. Me? I was a stowaway on a cruise ship, The *Hairy Fluke*. It stopped in Cuba, when they could do that, and I got on with fake documents, then jumped off when it stopped here. So if you're like that, welcome to the club."

"I'm new here," said Basil, "but I have no good story. I just need a safe place to stay."

Cheek sized him up with a look that showed he knew Basil was lying, but he let it go. "You can stay with me and my mother. She owns a shrimp trawler and let's the crew stay with her when they are sobering up. She always has crew jobs."

Basil said he didn't want to be a bother, but Cheek told him to hang up his apron and grab his duffle and follow him after he washed their plates. Basil didn't see any point in declining.

Ma welcomed him to her boat moored in the Key West bight marina. "Watch yer feet," she said as he stepped onboard. The odor reminded Basil of the night he slept in an alley near Crabby's Café Dumpster in the city. It wasn't the way Bunny's pillow fragranced his nostrils, but this would have to do.

Ma sized him up and disappeared down a hatch.

"She has a bunk for you, and work if you want it later this week. Rod is quitting shrimping too," said Cheek. "By then you'll have made enough at the joint to pay for bunk and board for the next couple of nights, then you can work it off shrimping after that."

Basil wasn't sure. Cheek scowled. "Look, man, you don't look like you have many options right now. Take it or we're done here."

Basil said, "I didn't mean to appear ungrateful. Of course. Thanks. Thanks a lot."

"Follow me," Cheek said. Basil, though glad to lie down for a change, found that his long legs hung over the end of the cot, making it hard for others, also staying in the cramped quarters, to pass him in the night.

Cheek told him not to eat Ma's breakfast because they could get it cheaper at work. Even though Cheek told him that his duffle was safe on the boat, Basil decided to take it with him. He didn't want Ma or the crew to rummage through it. Besides the crew was going out in the Gulf later that day and wouldn't return until morning. Basil wasn't sure of what he and Cheek would do all night when the restaurant closed, unless they decided to join them.

Basil tied the apron strings around his neck and waist. The island music was already on loud in the kitchen and he knew the prep for breakfast was under way. Cheek brought both of them strong Cuban coffee, reheated from the night before, and overcooked eggs and week-old toast. "You'll get used to it," he said, pouring hot sauce on both his eggs and toast. "Helps! Now to work. Dishes, breakfast, and bussing tables for breakfast, lunch and dinner."

Basil nodded. His hands were still sore from the hot water and strong soap. Other chores could be much better.

As the first sticky plates and crusty pans were delivered to his wash station, Basil readied himself. He was beginning to enjoy his new life, or interim to his former one. No Sangria. The chickens he had seen so far on the Key West streets squawked at a safe distance. Only one had flapped close enough to cause a sneeze. No Darwin and useless interns. No Mac. No family turning on him. No more bad books to be responsible for.

The breakfast and brunch crowd kept the restaurant full. At noon Cheek tapped him on the shoulder and said it was time to start bussing. He gave him a clean apron and instructions on how to balance a tray while picking up the dirty dishes. And he told him what to do to gather those dishes between courses. Basil practiced with a tray in the kitchen.

He pushed open the doors to the small eating area that led outside to a patio with giant fans and additional seating. *Not too bad,* he thought. He bussed a table of four and another, a two-top. With a flourish, he used a soapy rag to wipe the tables. The crowd kept coming in, a few at a time. Basil barely glanced at them. He just looked for the tables that needed to be wiped.

He rested for a few minutes inside the kitchen's screen door overlooking the shell parking area, when he saw the convertible pull in and park. A bright yellow Mustang. Three women wearing large sunglasses and matching flowered big-brimmed sun hats were inside. Basil froze. They got out. They looked around.

"Scruggy," said one.

"Yeah, but Mac said it was authentic."

Matt or Mac? Basil was in a panic. The women came toward the back door then realized they had to go to the front. "Let's sit outside," one said. "This looks really local. What fun." Basil trembled when he realized she sounded like Amanda.

Cheek pushed open the swinging doors. "Hey, man, get going. Tables to be bussed inside and out on the porch."

Basil looked around the kitchen and found a lost and found box. He grabbed a greasy Cuba Libra red baseball cap, which he pulled down so the brim covered his forehead. He found his sunglasses in his duffle and as Cheek returned to chastise him, Basil pushed past him with a tray.

"Don't be late again," Cheek muttered.

When he had finished clearing the inside tables, Basil took a deep breath and looked around the patio seating. There was only one recently vacated table near where the three women were seated and studying the menu.

He knew they would find little if anything vegan on the menu and regular food would be disappointing in this joint. He wondered what they were gabbing about, but it was hard to hear over the giant fans.

He backed up to the empty table, coming dangerously close to theirs, and turned slightly to grab two plates and tall glasses. He noticed

Shirley lift her sunglasses to stare at him. Shirley placed them back on her nose and said, "Amanda, before you get ready for the presentation tonight, let's take the Conch Train around town."

Basil hurried back to the kitchen without further glances in their direction.

He took another deep breath. He had been undetected for now, but they were now here in Key West, no doubt looking for him, and possibly Mac was here too. What presentation could his oldest daughter be giving in Key West of all places? Or was this trip just the vacation Shirley had always wanted?

The women left their conch fritters and shrimp salad untouched and returned to their convertible, with Amanda driving. Mora took a picture of the back of the restaurant before Basil, hands soapy, could duck out of view from his spot at the sink. Too far away, he hoped, for the camera to focus through the screen on his face. Besides, they wouldn't recognize him with the healthy beginnings of a beard and mustache. Mora had packed a razor in her kit of useful things, but he had never had used it.

Cheek startled him from behind. "Hey, stop oogling those chicks. They were asking about you so I told them you waz running from something."

Basil froze and hung on the sink.

"Just kiddin, man. I told them you were my brudda from Cuba and didn't speak English."

Basil didn't know if he should believe him.

"Ma just called and said she planned to shrimp tonight at ten, so we need to get there by 9:30. The boss here says we can leave at six. Didn't say why. You should go to Mallory Square to see the sunset. Big crowd, and crazy entertainment," Cheek continued.

Basil nodded. He'd have a few hours to get off his feet or look around a bit. At six, he hung up the apron, found his straw hat and duffle, and left the kitchen. Tourists were headed to the waterfront and he saw a schooner sailing away in the sunset. Afraid of bumping into his wife and daughters at such a popular spot, he wandered in the opposite direction on Duval Street. Posters for upcoming events and lost cats were tacked on posts and taped to windows. Numerous presumably lost cats darted in front of bicycles, and several chickens pecked at crumbs under patio tables. Basil stifled a sneeze. He looked in his duffle to see if Mora had thought to include tissues, and she had.

It was then that he noticed the poster taped to a decorative picket fence near a small area where artists were drawing caricatures and selling seashell jewelry. The poster was for a surprise reveal at a bookstore that evening for a new soon-to-be best-selling book written by the one and only Kenly Pope. It displayed the cover. Very professional, Basil had to admit.

So that's why Amanda is here. To promote Pope's book and the rest of the family came along for a vacation, he realized. Curious, he decided to find the bookstore and secrete himself nearby to see what was going on.

The sun was down and it was almost seven. Basil asked for directions from someone handing out discount coupons for drinks at the Hog's Breath Saloon. The bookstore was on a side street two blocks away. A light blue building with lime-green trim. Basil loped along Duval, noting that the boozy smell and occasional panhandler reminded him of the city he had left.

But as he sauntered along, he noticed that unlike the city, people here were talking and laughing, eating at outside tables and saying hi or smiling at strangers. The building were painted in colorful hues. And the air was filled with jasmine and a bush that smelled like orange blossoms. Flower vines covered porch railings. Amateur guitarists played Jimmy Buffet songs. Basil felt happier than he had in a long time. He wanted to take up painting or get a henna tattoo. Or pretend to smoke a Cuban cigar. He wanted to wear orange sandals.

Basil found that the bookstore was easy to spot. He stepped in the shadows across the street from it where he could observe. There was a surprisingly long line. Shirley and Mora were on the store's porch, handing out copies to those entering so customers would immediately bond with the book and take it inside for autographing.

He assessed his options. Obviously he couldn't join the line. There were open windows along the side, and thick, flowery bushes and dense palms near them. A good place to hide and listen. He carefully made his way across the street when nobody was looking, and struggled to get through the vines and branches, some prickly. His straw hat became ensnared so he decided to leave it behind for now.

His height was an advantage for once, and he could peer carefully through the hot pink bougainvillea into the open window.

The bookstore owner, well tanned and in her sixties, was wearing a flowered bright teal sundress. She beamed at those sitting and standing in the crowded room.

She welcomed the book lovers, apologized for the tight seating and lack of air-conditioning due to a malfunction earlier in the day, and she hoped the ceiling fans and open windows would provide relief. Then she said, "I'm Mirabella, and I am incredibly fortunate tonight to introduce you to the author of *The Devine Royalty Social Club Queen's Son* at the launch of this breakout novel. She will read from her book, and take questions plus, of course, sign copies at the conclusion. Put your hands together for Kenly Pope." Basil craned his neck to see the famed unknown author. To loud applause, a side door in the store opened and in stepped Amanda. Amanda? Where's Kenly? Maybe Amanda came along to introduce her. In the sudden hush, Amanda thanked everyone for coming out for the debut.

She smiled her lovely smile, looked at her mother and Mora standing in the back, and glanced briefly around the room, including at the windows, and said, "You are the first to know. I am Kenly Pope." There was a loud gasp and applause.

"I assumed a pen name because my father was the chief editor at my publishing house, and I didn't want to put him in a difficult position handling a manuscript with my real name on it. I wasn't sure if he would even like it. But I've been overwhelmed and gratified at the response. So I will read from the first chapter. The shopkeeper handed her a copy turned to the first page.

> "What'cha snitchin, Ashly Belor?"
> She looked surprised, but not as much as he might expect. "Nun yer business," said Ash. "Besides, it's not snitchin when nobody wants it."

Basil's eyes blurred. His beautiful Amanda. He was filled with longing to hug her, even if it was a terrible book. Then he felt something brush against his knee and a squawk. As he unsuccessfully tried to stifle an equally loud sneeze, he felt a stabbing, burning sting in his ankle from the prickly bush. He shouted *ouch,* and immediately regretted it as he crumpled; the bird briefly finding refuge on his shoulder, clucking. His throat closed and his eyes burned.

"Someone's hiding in the bushes," said a customer looking out. I see hair and a rooster. Call the police."

"No," said the storekeeper. "Drunks often get stuck there when they get lost. They find their way out."

Basil could feel his ankle swelling and itching. He sank closer to the ground, hoping that whatever had bitten him was gone.

Then hands grabbed under his arms. "Try to stand, Dad," said Mora.

"We've found you at last, Honeypie," said Shirley. "Here, lean on me."

"Can't walk. Ankle," said Basil, too overwhelmed to talk. He sneezed again and tried to rub his eyes.

"Sit over here," said Mora. She had found a lawn chair behind the store. "Oh my, I'll see if they have a first-aid kit."

Shirley rubbed his neck. "We need to talk. How about we go for a drinky-poo after Amanda's talk. Or we can go now and she can join us. We have so much to catch up on. Like, where you have been." Basil detected a change in tone—a sudden edge to her voice.

The hemp salve that Mora applied produced a dramatic reduction in swelling and pain. Basil reached for his duffle and said he thought he could make it to the Sea Urchin's Bar and Grille that they had suggested, which was only a block away. He could think of nothing to say. Nothing. Shirley and Mora raved about every flower, even moths visible in the street lights, and the full moon. The small eatery had six outdoor tables within a fenced enclosure adorned with strings of colored lights, and large fans for cooling. They had to wait for a table for four to be readied. Basil was grateful for a chance to sit. Shirley sat across from him, staring at his whiskered face. Shirley started a tab with ports for herself and Basil, and Mora asked for a Margarita.

"To the return of dear Basil," said Shirley waving her port toward him for a toast.

Basil felt numb. This was all so unexpected. Where he had been, and why? Such a blur. The port helped him relax, but it did not bring memories that he wanted to revisit.

Shirley downed half of her glass and said, "Basil, you don't seem ready to talk, but I'd like you to listen, and don't try to run again. I've talked with Dr. Porter Murff, who deals with professionals in crisis and he's agreed to treat you, I mean *you*, when we return. His initial appraisal is that you are suffering from Pre-retirement Depression Syndrome Triggered by Feathers. Very rare but also quite complicated."

Basil wanted to run. He wasn't sure what time it was, but Ma and Cheek would be waiting for him at the dock.

Mora gently placed her hand on his arm. "Dad, Shirley is right. I went with her to Dr. Murff, and he made a lot of sense. He went with us to court, and the charges against you were dropped. We talked with Mrs. Joyce Royce and she explained everything—that she didn't know you, except professionally. Then Shirley was devastated that she had left you in your time of need because of unwarranted suspicions. We had to find you!"

Basil wanted to believe them, and embrace them, but things seemed odd. Mora continued, "Sangria said you could have your job back for the next month, and no meetings in the chicken coop. See, everything will be okay, Dad. And Oscar Wilde can come home with a kitten of your choice. I desperately want a chance to get to know you, and Amanda wants to share her joy about a being a published author with you. You can sit with her at book signings."

Basil realized that the trap for his future was set.

"Please," pleaded Shirley. "You can keep your stupid, I mean grungy, beard. And if you want to keep that box with the embalmed kid in it, it's okay with the authorities."

Basil shuddered with the memory. He had another long sip. Shirley signaled the waiter for another round and four menus.

When Amanda arrived at 8:30, she rushed over to kiss Basil on the cheek.

"So glad you came to the program, Dad. We sold every one- as collector items. There were two people who bought copies because they heard someone reading the bound galley on your bus. What a hoot! And you, we've missed you terribly. Can't wait for you to come back home. Everything's arranged. Dr. Murff is a great help. Did Mom tell you that we have a flight arranged for tomorrow afternoon? This was going to be a fun family vacation, together at the yellow cottage but obviously we need to get back instead."

Basil glanced at the menu and thought. "This is all very sudden," he said finally. "I have to think about it."

"Think about what?" Shirley's voice became loud and treacherous. "After all that has gone on? Don't you know that we had to hire a detective and a lawyer to handle your bizarre case of bank robbery and grave theft so you could plead insanity, and set up hours of therapy and even bring Sangria in to get things settled at O.O&O.? Your thoughtless and insane behavior is more upsetting than menopause."

Mora grabbed Shirley's arm and whispered, "Calm down." Amanda made a zipper motion across her lips. Don't talk like that to Dad

"Well, I can say what I want, and he needs to listen," said Shirley. "This has just been such a wretched time for me and the girls, just when you were ready to retire and collect your bonus, and have that big party that Sangria was planning." She dabbed her weepy eyes.

Basil said, "What do you think things have been like for me?"

"That's what you need to talk about with Dr. Murff, that's his speciality, to sort out fantasy from reality," said Mora. "Wouldn't that be nice, Dad?"

He studied his wife and daughters, as the girls earnestly looked for his reaction to their plan to return home. He loved them. He missed Oscar Wilde. But he didn't trust their plan nor Dr. Murff. He knew reality very well.

"Why don't you all move down here? You always wanted to visit Key West, Shirley. Life is simpler. I like it." He accepted a third glass of port, and a plate of crab salad.

Shirley drummed her fingers on the table. "Dr. Murff said you might suggest that, but dagnabbit, Basil, you know that is fantasy not realism.

Amanda has her book career launched and Mora has a great job at the firm. And now again you only have a month to go. How can you support us bussing tables at that disgusting restaurant? I bet they've got you doing dishes. You look like a tramp, not the man I married, pretended to like his sonatas, served drinky-poos every night and . . . "

She would have continued but Amanda pounded on the table saying, "Mother! Stop it!"

Shirley glared and left angrily for the ladies' room, shouting, "I have no Plan C! Do you hear me, Basil? There is no Plan C! No Plans X Y or Z either!"

Basil signaled the waiter that he wanted his salad, with extra crackers, boxed to go.

"I'm tired from my travels, and need to get some rest," he said.

"Where are you going? Don't leave us, please. I'm sorry Mom sounded so cross, but we want to help you and get you back home. Where will you spend the night? We can all go back to the yellow house that Mora rented, then have breakfast together here tomorrow. We have so much to talk about. This place has great breakfast food, we hear," said Amanda

Basil stood. What he wanted to say wouldn't come out.

Mora said, "Dad, you shouldn't walk far on that ankle. I'll find a ride for you."

He looked at his daughters and then in the direction of the ladies' room, and shook his head. "Thanks, but never mind. I need to go. There's a lot to think about. I can make it on my own."

Amanda handed him his duffle. "See you at breakfast? Here? Nine?"

Basil nodded ambiguously. He hugged both daughters then left through the patio gate where a freshly painted lime-colored sedan with the word CAB, scrawled with a black marker on its back door was idling. He opened the door and slid in.

"Where to, Baz?" asked a familiar voice at the wheel. "You look like you need a shave and a haircut. Start a tab?"

Basil was too startled to answer. He tried to open the door to escape, but it locked.

Mac said, "C'mon, Baz, I'm starting a new CAB company and I need drivers. MacKeys Kabs. A key-lime theme. Maybe convertibles for tourists. You'll love it here. No one to bother you. Nobody telling you what to do or eat. Cats with extra toes are everywhere. SUNSETS, banned T-shirts, drag shows, you name it.

"Wiley's working on a new line of seashell ornaments. Tiny painted warthogs glued inside conch shells. He's even made an angel one that looks like Honey, you know the one I heard you liked the best. He's going to market them as from Warthog's Breath Saloon even if the Hog's Breath Saloon says it'll sue. He'll just MOVE his booth farther down the street or hawk them to tourists at Mallory Square. Wadya think, buddy?" Mac turned to see Basil's reaction.

"No warthogs for me. None. Done!" said Basil. He shook his head vigorously.

Mac shifted into drive and waited. "Like I SAID, you'll love it here."

The scent of jasmine filled the warm night air. Basil settled into the cracked leather seat. He thought a while, then smiled.

"Carpe diem."

The meter started.

Acknowledgments

Special thanks to wonderful people who provided encouragement, editing, criticism and suggestions in this long journey to complete this book. Especially to my patient and supportive husband, Jim, and those who confessed to laughing while reading, Denis Malloy, Abbie Grotke, Lenn Johns, Ph.D., and Sunny Agee. To Mark Zehr, our computer guru, who rescued the almost-finished manuscript from extinction when the hard drive died, and to our cats, who had their own ideas for keyboard insertions. And thanks to Keith Saunders, who used his immense talent to come up with the perfect cover design. And also to people in my life who unwittingly inspired several characters, and probably would prefer to remain unidentified. Some have pissed, I mean, passed away by now.

About the Author

Linda Salisbury has had a career in journalism and free-lance writing. She has written nineteen books, including twelve for children; several non-fiction; humorous novels and collections of humor columns that first appeared primarily in the Sarasota *Herald-Tribune*.

She is a cellist (self-taught violist, and has given up on piano despite many attempts), enjoys travel, and exercise on her three-wheel bike, and life in Florida with her husband, Jim, and their rescue cats, George Katz II and Tucker. And, she's immensely thankful for her great family and many wonderful friends.

Other Books by Linda Salisbury

Good-bye Tomato, Hello, Florida

Read My Lips, No New Pets

Smart Self-Publishing: An Author's Guide to Producing a Marketable Book (written with Jim Salisbury)

The Breezy Guide to Charlotte County, Florida (written with Jim Salisbury)

The Award-winning Bailey Fish Adventure Series
(For ages eight and up):

The Wild Women of Lake Anna

No Sisters Sisters Club

The Thief at Keswick Inn

The Mysterious Jamestown Suitcase

Ghost of the Chicken Coop Theater (read on Indiana Public Radio's Storyboard)

Trouble in Contrary Woods

Captain Calliope and the Great Goateenies

Treasure in Sugar's Bookbarn

Earthquake Surprise

Snooper Dude's Secret

What Could Go Wrong?

Mudd Saves the World: Booger Glue, Cow Diapers and other (not) Good Ideas (Ages seven and up)

But You Don't Look Funny (A collection of her best humor columns published in the Sarasota *Herald-Tribune*)

Mother's: A Novel of Hoarding, Friending and Mischief

The Sword and the Broom: The Exceptional Career and Accomplishments of John Mercer Langston